The Trial of Swords Hammers and Staves: Darkened Skies

Arush Gokul

Copyright © 2024 Arush Gokul

All rights reserved.

ISBN: 979-8-3329-5792-5

CONTENTS

1	A RABBIT IN DESPAIR	Pg 1
2	THE MOLES PROVIDENCE	Pg 4
3	THE SPAR	Pg 8
4	THE RAIDERS	Pg 13
5	RECOVERY	Pg 19
6	MOLE CITY	Pg 26
7	PATROL	Pg 49
8	THE PACKAGE	Pg 55
9	TRANSPORT	Pg 62
10	WELCOME TO VORTEX CITY	Pg 75
11	PREPARATION	Pg 79
12	HOW TO TAUNT A DRAGON	Pg 91
13	FALLEN	Pg 100
	EPILOGUE	Pg 106

ACKNOWLEDGMENTS

I want to talk about everyone who has contributed to my book. Simon, your ideas and unwavering positivity have been helpful. Juan, your helpful contributions have enhanced the content significantly. Vitor, your planning has shaped the structure of the book. Carson, thank you for reading my book early and giving feedback. Sakish, your belief in my work has been crucial. Llyah, I appreciate your feedback which has helped my ideas thrive. Alex, your amazing ideas have made a huge impact. Ishaan, your support has meant the world to me. Cristiano, thank you for your insightful feedback. Special thanks to Arvaan, for being the first to believe in my book. Xavier, your creative characters have brought my story to life in unexpected ways. Jorge, thank you for your support and for sparking the initial idea. Daniel, your belief has kept me motivated. Mary, your help in drawing pictures to envision my book and early readership are greatly appreciated. Mila (Juan's cat), your presence in my book has added charm. Aadithya, thank you for drawing pictures. Arthur, your extreme positivity was extremely helpful to writing my book. Each of you has played a crucial role in helping me write my book, and I am deeply grateful for your support and contributions.

1 A RABBIT IN DESPAIR

It was a wonderful day in the continent of Viscland, home to humanoid creatures with bustling cities, blue skies, and green grass. One Rabbit, mainly Ark, was sleeping in his current class. His teacher called on him, "So Ark, could you please expand the equation $(2x+4)(4x+3)$?" Ark woke from his deep slumber and said, "You woke me up for math? I must be dreaming!" The whole class laughed. The teacher sighed, but he was cut short. The bell rang, and the teacher sighed again as the class ran out.

Ark was an ordinary bunny with extraordinary intelligence. His classmates often mocked him for his stupidity, but Ark ignored the rude comments. Ark ran back to his house, but before that, he went to his best friend's house, his name was Arvaan. Arvaan is one of the most robust rabbits in Bunny Town. Ark knocked on his door, and a Rabbit with pulsing muscles answered; it was Arvaan. "Yo, what's good, bro," he said, giving Ark a complicated handshake. "Hi, Arvaan. Do you have any carrots?". Ark thought that carrots were one of the only reasons to live. "No bro, carrot. co has stopped shipping," said Arvaan. "Oh no!" responded Ark, terrified;

Carrot. Co happened to be Ark's favorite all-organic carrot brand. "Why?" said Ark. "I think it's because of the recent harsh weather near their company. Horses are running scared," replied Arvaan. "Interesting," said Ark. "Well, what should we do?"

For once in his life, Arvaan looked stumped. "I... I don't know." Ark and Arvaan's one-hour schedule of eating carrots was ruined without carrots. After this, they played a few games, sparring with swords, and had fun. Still, the weather had ruined their day. "How about we eat some mushroom stew?" suggested Arvaan. Ark sighed but reluctantly agreed. Arvaan began heating some stew on the fire.

"How about we go to carrot.co ourselves to try and get some carrots?" asked Ark. "That's an interesting thought," replied Arvaan. "Carrot. Co is extremely far from here, so we would need swift horses, which cost lots of allos."

Allos was the currency of the world of Viscland. They come in gold coins, silver coins, and bronze coins. Ark had very pitiful bronze allos in the depths of his piggy bank. Arvaan had won countless medals and prizes for strength in his town, but most of that money went to taxes for Lunaria. Lunaria is the capital of the rabbits and home to the king. Ark knew that only the rich people lived there. While Ark was pondering what he could do for money (possibly open a soup store with Arvaan), Arvaan had been doing his research. There were papers all over the floor on how to bargain well and papers about good horses to buy. "This is absurd. Two hundred fifty allos for a mediocre horse?" said Arvaan, crestfallen. "Surely that's to buy, right?" asked Ark. "why can't we just rent one you ask? We could but wait till you see the best horses come from a city that's far away." "They only accept people who are good at fighting," replied Arvaan. "Oh no." said Ark, "That's not even the worst part. The cost is unfathomable for us," said Arvaan. He was in a bad mood like Ark because all rabbits liked carrots. Without it, their lives felt incomplete. The two pondered about what felt like ages on what to do. It wasn't just them; the whole town was sad about not having carrots. Some even claimed that they would attack the carrot company. The company is being threatened just because of the carrots.

Then, it hit Arvaan like lightning. "I have an idea!" he exclaimed; Ark was eagerly listening now.

"We will ask my friend Daniel Zorko; he's a smart mole who lives in Stone Haven. We can walk there; he'll know what to do."

There were three races in Viscland. They joined together to form peace, but it didn't last long. People fought over natural resources and leaders with greed and envy etched in their minds. One of these races was the moles, who were extremely good at building and physical strength.

Ark packed his bag and got ready to leave. "Goodbye, Bunny town; I hope I'll be back soon," he said as he ran to catch up with Arvaan.

2 THE MOLES PROVIDENCE

Ark had been journeying for almost 15 minutes now when Arvaan queried, "I wonder why Carrot Co got delayed. We make them the most profit, and they still have some carrots in the higher-level towns."

"What?" Asked Ark perplexed

"You don't pay attention in school, do you? You don't even know about the war that is going on?"

"What war?" replied Ark.

Arvaan, sighing again, asked, "Have you heard about the terrifying general who is threatening to take over the world?" His voice trembled.

"No," replied Ark, unease creeping over him.

"Well," explained Arvaan, "he's a formidable leader who desires global power. He started a war because of his insatiable hunger for power."

"What a greedy guy," said Ark.

"Unfortunately, many people believe in his rule and that he should be all-powerful. I heard he'd raided some of the main mole areas," responded Arvaan.

"Such as?" asked Ark.

"Stone Watch Depths," replied Arvaan.

Ark had heard of Stone Watch Depths; it was the one class he could remember in which he did not fall asleep. It had advanced siege weaponry like ballistae and trebuchets to launch flaming rocks towards the enemy. The raiders also had to deal with their 20-foot-tall stone walls while they were burning; they would fire the ballistae for certain death.

"So, how did they raid it?" asked Ark.

"So, this is the one class in which you were awake," said Arvaan. "Well, they raided by having an advantage nobody expected."

"What was it?" asked Ark.

"Potions, some of the best-brewed ones I've ever seen. They gave strength, speed, and fire resistance to dodge the boulders. The moles outnumbered the Raiders almost 2 to 1 and still lost. Now, their city is in shambles. Diamond Citadel is also shelling out a lot to get that city repaired. It was one of the best cities in the rank 3 zone."

"Why shell out so much?" asked Ark.

"Stone Watch Depths was famous for housing moles of good strength, and it was the easiest center of crafting to reach. Traders would come from all over to get great armor and weapons. It generated too much revenue to be ignored. So, Diamond Citadel is paying for the reconstruction."

They continued to chat about the war for the next hour, but then they ran out of ideas, resorting to making bad puns for the rest of the trip.

"Alright, I got one," said Ark. "Want to rock out?" Ark pointed towards the rock. Arvaan's expression remained solid as stone. Then Arvaan said, "Want to join the club?" He pulled out a golf club from his bag. Ark winced at the terrible pun. Then Ark said, "Don't go barking up the wrong tree." He pointed towards a tree. Arvaan couldn't help but laugh at this. "That's enough," he said with a pained expression. "So, what do we talk about now?"

"Anything but puns," replied Arvaan.

"Alright, let's talk about what class you want to become."

"I don't want more classes," said Ark.

"No, not that, silly," said Arvaan. "What class do you want to become, like a warrior, mage, rogue, or archer?"

Ark didn't say anything but gave a confused look.

"Well, it makes sense that you don't know. They only teach you about it in the rank 2 zone," replied Arvaan. "At Stone Haven, we can go to school again, and you could learn more about the situation. Until you know about that, let me say, I want to become a warrior."

"Wow, very cool," said Ark, pretending to understand what he was saying.

They continued to chit-chat until, before they knew it, they had arrived. They saw a giant tower followed by a short stone wall.

It looked like they found themselves in a tense situation, surrounded by a voice, "STAND DOWN," said the voice. They were in a tense situation before they could recognize what was happening, surrounded by warriors wielding axes, hammers, and even a dagger.

"LAY DOWN YOUR WEAPONS," boomed the voice.

3 THE SPAR

"Um, we have none," blurted Ark. The warriors realized something was wrong. Ark and Arvaan were unarmed. "Wait, they are unarmed. They speak the truth," said the warriors. "Lower your weapons," responded the voice. Everyone lowered their weapons. Then, a cool-looking mole with amazing-looking armor walked out. "My apologies. We are just on edge after what happened at Depth Stone Watch. It was one of the most heavily armored forts in the rank 3 zone. Still can't believe they lost with all that weaponry," said a warrior in the pact.

"They lost because a rogue rabbit from the rank 4 zone sold them overpowered potions and stat-boosting food. At least, those are the rumors."

"Why blame it on the rabbits and not those stinking Sylvanites?"

"Because we've been over this," replied the leader. "Only rabbits specialize in potions, food, and relationships. Sylvanites could not produce potions near the caliber of the potions used on the raid." The guard who said that lowered his head.

Ark said, "So, can we come in? What business do you have here anyway, rabbit? I'm curious."

"Well, we're here to talk to Daniel Zorko," said Ark. Everyone laughed. "He's our best scientist. Like most moles, he's good at technology but bad at magic. Only high-ranking officers can talk to him. What do you want to ask him?"

"I'm going to ask him if we can have a fast method of transportation," Ark added quickly.

"If you want to get in here, you must prove yourself."

"How?" asked Ark.

"Don't worry," said Arvaan. "I'll handle this," pushing Ark aside. "Sir, what is your name?" he asked the Captain.

"Ah, how rude of me. My name is Arthur, and I am the Captain of Stone Haven. We supply recruits every day to the higher zones. Stone Haven serves as the training grounds of novice moles, and we fear getting raided by the Iron Tyrant's armies."

"Interesting," said Arvaan. "We need to see Daniel Zorko to get to Carrot Co because Ark and I love carrots."

The thought of carrots made Ark drool.

"If you want to prove yourself access to my city, I will test you with a test of strength."

"How?" said Arvaan.

"Not you." The Captain pointed towards Ark.

"What kind of test, sir?" Ark asked, a bead of sweat forming on his forehead.

"I shall allow you to spar with anyone here, and if you can beat them, you can access the city. If not, you will never be welcome here," his voice boomed.

Then Ark pointed a long finger towards the Captain. "You." He said, "I want to spar with you."

Everyone let out a booming laugh.

"You fight the Captain," said a warrior. "You will get creamed," said another. "He is one of the strongest moles in the zone, so he is our Captain."

Arvaan crouched next to Ark. "This is a bad idea, Ark. You know that moles are naturally stronger than rabbits, right?"

"I do not care. If the moles want strength, I'll prove it to them."

"Ark, let me handle this. I am stronger than you, and you know it," said Arvaan.

"Nuh-uh!" said Ark.

They continued to bicker back and forth, their voices growing steadily louder until Arthur said, "I grow weary of your constant bickering."

At last, Arvaan gave up fighting, so Ark got ready to fight.

"I am going to destroy you," said Arthur.

"Wait," Captain Arthur said to a warrior. "What is it, Sara?" the Captain said.

"Well, it seems unfair that you have a weapon, but the bunny doesn't have a weapon."

"Hmmm, fetch the weapon chest," said Arthur, pointing a finger at two of his warriors.

"Right away, sir," they responded, speeding off behind the high stone walls of Stone Haven.

"Wow, this guy must have some authority," Ark thought.

The soldiers quickly returned five minutes later, carrying a large chest. They put it down on the grass and looked at it greedily.

"Can I open it?" he asked.

"Knock yourself out," replied the Captain.

"Thank you," said Ark. He opened it and saw the most glorious weapons he had ever seen.

Arthur said, "That's the might and precision of mole engineering and crafting."

Ark looked into the chest. He felt like a bunny in a carrot store. Ark saw many weapons: a hammer, an axe, knuckles, a rapier, a mace, and a basic sword. He grabbed the basic sword because he had no idea how to use the other weapons effectively.

"Ah, I see you've chosen the path of the sword," said the Captain. "I, however, chose the path of the hammer." He pulled out a one-handed hammer.

Ark thought the hammer looked menacing, but the Captain noticed him looking over it. "Like it?" Arthur said. "Some of the finest moles in this zone crafted it for me. It was made of the finest materials in Stone Haven."

"It looks menacing," said Ark.

"Are you still sure you want to fight?" said the Captain. "You look worried."

Ark knew he had to represent strength, so he bravely said, "I'm ready."

"We need a judge," said Arvaan, popping in.

"You be the judge," Arthur said instantly.

"Okay, I shall review the basic sparring rules," said Arvaan. "As soon as I say start, we begin. There will be no killing, and the other side wins when the opponent surrenders the match. Ready your positions."

Ark got into a fighting position, wielding his sword. The Captain got into his fighting stance, wielding his hammer in one hand. Looking extremely strong, Arvaan said, "Alright, 3, 2, 1," and at that moment, a horn sounded.

Ark dashed at the Captain, but the Captain blocked quickly and said, "WAIT, THAT'S NOT THE STARTING BELL."

Ark skidded to a halt. Then, a mole came running out of Stone Haven. He finally reached them and said, "Captain, the raiders are here!"

"Oh, my this will be quite a fight," said Arthur.

4 THE RAIDERS

"Instruct all soldiers to report to their stations and get those siege weapons running at once!"

"Yes, Sir," the mole darted off.

"This fight will have to wait; the city is under siege." Ark wiped an eyebrow, slightly pleased he did not have to battle the captain.

Everyone ran to Stone Haven and got on top of the walls.

"Grab a bow," ordered the captain. Ark hastily grabbed a bow and overheard the captain talking with his lieutenant.

"Sir, the raiders are well-armored and have battering rams."

"Who is the leader of the team?" asked Arthur.

"Captain Mila, one of the last living members of the cat race. She's a rogue and a good one."

"Alright, everyone, watch out for the captain's tricks," said Arthur. "Rogues can be tricky."

Ark didn't understand what he was hearing, but whatever it was, it was a problem.

Once Ark and Arvaan grabbed bows, they looked over the wall and saw an army approaching.

"Woah," both Arvaan and Ark said.

"Stop admiring them and start firing if you do not want to end up as rabbit soup!"

"Yes, Sir," they both responded.

They began to fire arrows and saw a glinting soldier with shiny armor in the front.

"That must be the captain," said Arvaan.

"I don't think so," replied a voice behind them. It was Arthur. "Rogues are known for low health and trickery. I highly doubt she's on the front lines. Daniel, have you got those siege weapons running yet?" He looked towards a scrawny-looking mole.

"Almost, Sir," said the mole.

"Wait, you're Daniel?" sputtered Ark.

"Yes, that is me, alright, but whatever you want will have to wait." He gestured towards the army outside.

Then, they all saw a metal contraption on wheels.

"What is that?" asked Arvaan.

"Invention number 456, cannon," answered Daniel.

"You haven't changed a bit," Arvaan grinned.

"This is what's going to help us." He pointed the cannon into the crowd. "3, 2, 1, FIRE!" said Daniel. The cannon fired a large metal sphere that struck a vast crowd, turning at least 15 soldiers into dust.

"Wait, why did they turn to dust?" asked Ark.

"The Iron Tyrant's twisted experiments," replied Captain Arthur. "He created a spell to turn his armies into dust on defeat, to make sure we don't get the spoils of the weaponry."
"Ohhh," said Ark.
"Bah, you're awful with a bow. Come with me to aid the cavalry," said Arthur.
Ark went outside. He heard swords clashing and arrows flying. Then Arthur said, "There's the captain! Ark, I'll cover for you. Engage the captain!"
Ark dashed towards the soldier in shiny armor. His sword connected with her perfectly, and then she turned into a log.
"What?" said Ark.
"BEHIND YOU!" yelled Arthur, but it was too late. Her thin sword had hit Ark directly. Ark was on the floor now. The captain walked towards him.
"Well, well, well," said Mila. "They sent an amateur to get me."
"H-How is it that you can turn into logs and teleport behind me?" croaked Ark.
"What? Ever heard of a base class, amateur?" she explained.
"What? Turning into a log or teleporting?" asked Ark.
"Both," Mila answered with a grin. "Now it's time I finish you off." She grabbed her thin sword and pointed it towards Ark's face. "I shall make this a quick and painless death." She got ready to attack, and then BOOM! A shot was fired from the cannon and struck Mila directly.

"Woah," said Ark.

Mila was surprisingly alive, but her armor had seen better days; it was full of cracks.

"FINISH HER OFF!" BELLOWED DANIEL holding off some enemies.

Ark didn't need someone to tell him twice. He dashed towards the captain, who now lay wounded on the ground, and then he said, "Time for payback." He raised his sword unsteadily, prepared to strike, and boom! The captain turned into a log. Ark revolted in horror. "Oh no, NOT AGAIN, NOT TWICE!"

"OH YES," REPLIED MILA, who had directly hit Ark again with her thin sword. Ark started to bleed. She stomped over Ark's face. "Hmmm, I'm hungry. Got any food?" The captain took Ark's bag and began to look for food. "Oooh, carrots," she replied.

Ark gasped. "I didn't even know I had any left," he thought. She began to eat the carrots, and Ark remembered the sweet aroma and taste of carrots. "NOOOO! YOU WILL NOT EAT MY CARROTS!" He stood up incredibly fast as if he was immune to the pain of his previous attacks. He dashed at Mila, sword raised at blazing speeds. Mila tried to defend with her sword, but the attacks were too fast.

"How is this possible?" she said. Ark struck fiercely at the spots in her armor with cracks in it. Soon, the armor broke and fell into pieces.

"NOOOOOOOOO!" She yelled. "DO YOU HAVE ANY IDEA HOW EXPENSIVE THAT WAS, YOU NOOBLET?!"
Ark didn't care. He was moving faster than ever. All the archers and enemy soldiers watched in awe as the captain got obliterated by Ark.
"Fine, take the carrots, you glutton," said Mila, exasperated. Ark paused and then realized what he had done. "Oh my." He picked up the carrots and began to eat. Then, he decided to check on the captain. The whole battle had come to a halt as everyone was watching.
"Why do you work for the Iron Tyrant?" asked Ark.
"Because he's the only one who would offer help. My village was in ruins," she said, "families unable to feed their young ones. I had to step up and work for him. He would provide the village with protection. In exchange, we had to join his army."
"Step away from his wrath," said Ark. "I will try to help your village the best I can, but please order your troops to surrender and help end this war."
She contemplated the decision and said, "Yes, I'll join you."
Ark reached out a hand. "Now join us." She reached out her hand to grab Ark's, and then there was a loud whistle. A arrow had fired. It hit Mila directly, and she was now dust. Ark looked around; this was no trick. She was dust. But when he looked to see who fired the shot, it shocked him to see Milas' own teammate standing with a crossbow
"Traitors never prosper," said the soldier.

Ark looked at him, but then Ark felt a sharp pain in his chest. The wounds had caught up to him; he fainted to the sound of "Retreat! Retreat!"

5 RECOVERY

Two days later...

Ark awoke in a strange room. "W-where am I?" Ark croaked. He was overwhelmed by pain and the smell of potions. The room was very fancy, sporting a nice red carpet and seeming to have suitable medical devices. Ark could make out the silhouettes of three people.

"His recovery is faster than expected," said one of the shadowy figures. "I'm surprised Ark stood up to the captain like that."

"Pah, please," said one of the voices. "He only won because of my cannon."

"Where am I?" said Ark.

"You're in the Stone Haven Hospital," said one of the figures. "My name is Amy. I'm the doctor, and you seem to be doing well."

At once, Ark remembered everything that happened in the fight. He recalled that one of the soldiers had killed Mila. "ARTHUR, where is the one who killed her?" demanded Ark, "he killed Mila for no reason; she was going to side with us."

"I'm right here, Ark," said Arthur, no longer wearing his armor. He still looked tough, though. Ark saw Arthur Walk towards him.

"Maybe it's for the better we must never let the Iron Tyrant's minions' side with us. They show deception and malice. She threatened the city, Ark."

"I don't believe you. We could have sided with the captain; she could have helped us bring down the Iron Tyrant's army."

Arthur shook his head. "You remind me of when I was younger. Always thinking you could be friends with anyone, and you know what? I was a naïve fool, and you're acting like one now."

Ark sat up and was about to stride out of the room.

"WAIT, I have not yet cleared you for duty," said Amy, scowling. Ark sat back down; he wanted to leave this town, but even he knew he was too weak. The blows hit him hard, and there was no one good enough to brew health potions, as only the rabbits specialized in it. So, the recovery would be slow. He decided to go back to sleep.

Ark awoke three hours later to Arvaan staring at him. Ark sat up straight and noticed he had casts all over him. It looked to him that the injuries were more severe than he thought.

"The doctor has a message for you. You're cleared for duty."

"Hooray," Ark said sarcastically. He felt clear for duty, but getting around would be a challenge. Ark stood up, and to his surprise, he felt almost normal. Of course, there was pain here and there, but nothing he couldn't handle.

"Um, Ark, I think we may have a problem," said Arvaan.

"What is it?" said Ark.

"Well, I think you should see it yourself." He pulled the curtain, blocking the window down. Instantly, Ark got blasted by sunlight.

"OH NO, THE SUN IS GOING TO KILL US ALL," Ark cried. Even Arvaan was noticing how intense the sun was. They had both been in windowless rooms for a day.

"No, not that silly," said Arvaan. It took a few minutes, but Ark's eyes eventually adjusted to the sunlight, and then he noticed a loud commotion. Looking out the window, he saw hundreds of people gathered outside, along with a wood podium and a well-dressed mole standing atop it. Ark assumed it was the mayor. The crowd held microphones- it was one of Daniels's newest inventions. If you said something in one, your voice would be amplified, and the only sales he had made were to news reporters. That was what Ark had concluded, but even more surprising was that the reporters were not just moles but also rabbits.

"I still don't see the problem," said Ark. "What are they reporting anyway?" he asked.

"I can answer both your questions with one answer," Arvaan said firmly.

"Oh no," said Ark. He thought to himself why they were reporting him, and he couldn't come up with any reason, so he asked Arvaan. Arvaan noted that it was because he defeated the captain.

"No one had ever seen anything like it. You destroyed the captain in a few moves. It was marvelous to watch. He said that because you're so strong, everyone, including me, wants to know how you did it." He added.

Ark thought back to the battle, but it made him sad to think about Mila, who had lost her life. Could Ark blame CaptainArthur though? He thought harder and harder. No, he couldn't blame him. He thought he was being careful. It's the Iron Tyrant he should blame and that stupid soldier. He started the war. He always didn't like the idea of him ruling over since he heard of him, but this fueled his anger further. Arvaan noticed Ark staring blankly.

"Um, are you okay?" said Arvaan.

Ark snapped back to reality. "Yeah, I'm fine," he said, but he felt angry with the Iron Tyrant. He vowed he would one day put him to justice.

"Well, whether we like it or not, we will have to face the crowd soon," Ark sighed as he and Arvaan walked down the hallway and out of the building. Mustering all his courage, he stepped beyond the doors and was immediately surrounded by news reporters. The commotion was much louder now. Ark saw a microphone shoved in his face.

"How is it that you beat the captain, Ark?" one of the news reporters asked.

"Well, I just swung my sword until I got mad, then I swung my sword more, and the cannon turned her to dust," the reporter said. He looked extremely disappointed, but before he could respond, four moles in armor with massive shields surrounded Ark.

"We have orders from the mayor to protect you," said the moles. Ark could hear the clamoring and shouting of the reporters. "I got here first. I should be the one to interview him," shouted one. "We all got here simultaneously," the other one yelled back. It was extremely noisy.

Ark turned around to see that Arvaan was gone. He assumed that he had gotten lost in the crowd. He looked at the crowd. This was different from what he desired. All Ark ever wanted was carrots and to make more friends. He didn't want to be a hero. He knew most people would love to be a hero, but he wasn't most people.

Ark looked around again. There were still many reporters outside, all shoving each other for a chance to get close, but the guards had been protecting Ark with the shields so no one could question him. Ark thought it was a warzone outside, even though he had just been in one. Ark somehow found this worse as the guards inched toward where the mayor stood. Ark began to take in how small the city was. Also, to his confusion,

Arvaan had told him the moles lived underground, not above ground. Ark made a mental note to ask him next time.

Ark and the moles finally reached the stage where the mayor was standing. The guards finally dropped their shields and walked towards the mayor.

"It's good to see you," said one of the moles.

"Likewise," replied the mayor. Ark didn't know what to say, so he responded with a friendly "Hi."

The mayor just looked at him before replying, "Ah, you must be Ark. I've heard so much about you, the legendary idiot who beat up the captain of the raiding party."

"That's me," Ark replied. Although Ark thought the mayor calling him an idiot was rude, he kept it to himself.

"The audience wants your information. How did you defeat the captain?" he asked.

"I got mad, then I felt faster and won the fight. The cannon helped, though."

The mayor looked crestfallen as if he wanted the answer: "I ate a crystal in a magic cave that gave me powers; boy, you need to understand; some people need help in this world. We need to know if you have a secret for fighting; cities go down daily, and we need power more than ever!" he replied.

"Even with the cannon, you stood no chance against her," making his voice louder so the crowd heard him. The mayor shook his head.

"Even our captain would have struggled against her, and moles are far stronger than rabbits."

Ark shrugged. "I don't know what else to tell you," the mayor said. "Ark, I've heard you want to talk to Daniel Zorko."

Ark's eyes lit up. "Yes, I want to talk to him," Ark said.

The mayor smiled. "Now, under normal circumstances, Daniel is extremely busy. Only high-ranking officials can talk to him because he's the head scientist, but since your friend Arvaan is friends with him and you nearly saved the city, I think I can make an exception. I'll schedule an appointment with him quickly."

"Thanks so much," said Ark.

"No problem, Ark. I want our hero to be able to talk with anyone in our city. Why are you talking to him anyway?"

"I need him to help us get a method of transportation so I can go to Carrot. Co," said Ark.

"Interesting," said the mayor. "I heard they stopped shipping because they got raided by the Iron Tyrant's forces," said the mayor.

"So that's what happened," said Ark.

"They are using carrots as supplies to feed his army," continued the mayor, "but good luck getting there. It's far away in a superior position. I think their leader is a fencer."

Ark looked at the mayor blankly. "So you haven't even been educated on how the world works. It's time I sent you to our school."

6 MOLE CITY

Ark had gone with the mayor through the town until they reached a tiny house.

"Is this your house?" said Ark, surprised.

"It's the elevator," said the mayor.

Ark was about to ask him what that meant when suddenly the doors opened, and inside was a colossal elevator. Probably ten people were already in it, but they were glad to make room for the mayor and Ark. The mayor then flicked a switch, and the elevator descended. As Ark was going down, he heard several people murmuring.

"Is that Ark the hero?" asked a child to his mom.

"Yes, dear," replied the mom.

Once they finally reached the bottom, Ark got a better view of things. His eyes widened. He could smell coal and feel the heat, but what he saw around him amazed him. It was a giant city at least three times as big as Bunny Town. The mayor looked at Ark's widened eyes and chuckled.

"This cavern is our actual city," he said to Ark. The mayor and Ark continued walking until Ark saw a magnificent-looking house. It looked like it had been a boulder once, but it had sleek marble pillars and a nice red carpet.

"Wow," said Ark. "This is your house?"

"Indeed," said the mayor, "Come on in." Ark came in and went to the guest room. It was nicer than any room they had ever had at Bunny Town. The room walls looked like they were made from stone, giving it an earthy vibe.

"All right, Ark. I'll send you to school in the morning. You're lucky they are just starting the first unit." Ark didn't respond. He looked at some of the paintings like a giddy child.

"Who's that?" said Ark, pointing to a painting. The figure was a mole wearing glasses and a lab coat. He looked much more innovative than anyone Ark had ever seen.

"The person right there is named Mr. Aguinava. He used to work for one of our top cities, specifically the technological development center, which is the top one in all of our Molevern cities. He was the head scientist of the whole town. Some argue that Aguinava is the best Molevern scientist."

"Cool," said Ark.

"Unfortunately, the Iron Tyrant's minions captured our brilliant scientist on a trip to Stone Watch Depths, which, as you know, was raided."

"Doesn't he have guards? After all, he is crucial," said Ark.

"That's the thing. Aguinava had some of the finest guards surrounding him. We don't know how he got captured, but our intel says he's at Grim Keep. Oh, look at the time," said the mayor. "You better get off to bed. You have a big day tomorrow." The mayor blew out the lantern and closed the door. Ark fell asleep when he hit the bed, thinking about what Grim Keep was.

Ark woke up the following day, brushed his teeth, and dressed. He was finally going to learn what all those fancy words meant. "If only I hadn't slept in class," Ark thought. Ark went to the school with the mayor. Like the other buildings, it was made of rock. The one thing Ark didn't like about Stonehaven was that there was no sunlight underground. He made it inside the school. As the teacher was about to start, he sat at a desk next to a few other moles. On the board, he saw "Day One Topics: EXP, Stats, Primary Classes."

"Okay, class," he said, looking back at everyone. "As you have already seen, we will review EXP, stats, basic classes, tiered cities, and professions today. First, let me tell you about EXP; EXP is the magic imbued to change our classes. The higher your level of EXP, the stronger you will be."

"How do we know how much experience we have right now?" a mole in front of Ark said.

"Well, this is where the magic part comes in. I want you all to concentrate on the word EXP." Ark tried concentrating on it. They did this for about 15 minutes until Ark finally saw a screen pop up in front of him. It was the most bizarre thing. He tried to put his hand through it, but it passed right through. It looked to Ark as though it was a hologram. At this point, everyone had gathered around him, looking at his screen.

"Woah," said Ark as he looked closer. "It says I'm level 3." There was a ton of other information on the screen, but Ark decided to process it later.

"Oh wait, how do I close the screen?" he said to the teacher.

"Concentrate on the word 'close,'" he said without looking at Ark. So Ark concentrated on the word "close," and just as soon as it appeared, it was gone.

The teacher looked towards Ark. "You managed to get your first screen in 15 minutes. Most take 30," he said in awe.

"I guess I'm just that good," replied Ark, shrugging. Then Ark had a thought.

"What's your name?" he said to the teacher.

"Oh, how rude of me. My name is Mr. Winston, but you can call me Wins."

"Okay, Wins," said Ark, shrugging.

"Okay, everyone, now that everyone knows how EXP works, let's talk about ways to earn it. These ways include any strenuous activity, though some award more than others. For example, fighting will give you much more EXP than jogging," said Wins.

"So that must be how I got so much EXP," Ark thought.

"Apart from looking at your screen, you can also look at others by looking at them and concentrating on the word 'screen' while looking at another person," continued Mr. Wins. So Ark tried concentrating on a solid mole in front of him. After a few minutes, only the same screen came up in front of him.

"Wow, you got the hang of this fast, much faster," he said in a quieter voice. Ark ignored Mr. Wins, looking at the same screen he saw. Still, Ark noticed the numbers were much more extensive.

"Interesting," Ark asked. He asked if the numbers were more significant because he was stronger than me. We will understand these numbers in the following topic: your stats or statistics.

"The first one is strength, or STR, as an abbreviation."

"This is silly. You don't need an abbreviation for strength," thought Ark to himself.

"The STR stat is a stat that tells you how strong you are physically and how much damage you can do; the more you have, the better. For example," he looked at a mole in the front row and used the scanner on him. "What's your name?" asked Wins to the kid.

"Ricardo."

"Well, Ricardo, you have a strength stat of 12," said the teacher enthusiastically. "That's a mighty good number for your level, which is 2, but that number makes sense because moles are usually the strongest out of all three races."

"Three?" Ark said, confused.

"Yes, three," replied Mr. Winston, "rabbits, moles, and those blasted sylvinites, but that's a topic for another day. So, let's get back to this topic. Next, we have agility or AGI." He wrote on the chalkboard. "This stat reflects speed, agility, or overall nimbleness. This stat also reflects evasion chances. Rabbits are the best at this as they are swift compared to the other races." The class turned to see Ark, and they all used their screens on him.

"Woah, that's a lot," said one of the moles.

"Impressive," replied Winston. Ark didn't know what they were talking about until he pulled up his screen to see the number 15 under agility.

"Woah, even I didn't know I was that agile." A few years ago, Ark remembered that Arvaan had tried chasing him across the whole town because he forgot to pay the electricity fees, but Arvaan didn't even get close enough to catch him.

"That number is impressive," said Winston, "even for a rabbit. What level are you again, Ark?"

"3, sir."

"Indeed, that number is fine, Ark. Let me try something." As he said this, Winston picked up a jar and threw it at Ark.

"THINK FAST!"

Ark ran out of the way super quickly, avoiding the shattering glass.

"What was that for?!" exclaimed Ark.

Winston chuckled. "I wanted to see how fast your reflexes are, and they seem just as good as it says."

"What about the mess?" said Ark.

"It's fine." Then he muttered some incantations, and the glass floated into the garbage. The whole class stared in amazement.

"WHAT?!" exclaimed Ark, as did the whole class. Once the crowd settled down, Mr. Winston explained it was telekinesis, a form of magic that allows the user to pick things up; although there is a supposed weight limit of pounds, even for skilled mages, that's as high as it goes.

"So you're a magician of some sort?" asked Ark.

"Well, the proper term is a mage, but yes, I am a mage, so even if you had gotten hurt from the glass, I could heal you right up."

"I see," said Ark impressed. "Let's move on to the next skill, intellect or INT. This skill tells you your thinking skill, wits, and quick thinking, and affects spellcasting and magic. Take my telekinesis, for example. The higher my INT, the stronger it will be. It also affects battle strategies."

"Interesting," Ark thought to himself. "Everyone use their screens on me." So, everyone did as instructed.

"Wow, 32," said someone. "That's so smart."

Winston said, "Oh, you're embarrassing me. It's not that high for my level."

"What's your level?" asked someone.

"Nine," Winston said sheepishly.

"Only?" another asked.

"Well, as the progression goes on, it gets harder and harder to get a higher level. And anyway, I'm only about a few years older than you lot. We must move on to the next skill, vitality or VIT. This skill represents how much of a beating you can take. Moles typically have higher vitality than rabbits or sylvinites."

"There's that word again. I wonder who sylvinites are," Ark thought to himself. Winston noticed Ark drifting off and called on him.

"Would you like to share anything with the class, Ark?"

"Yes," said Ark, "what's a sylvinite?"

Winston was taken aback by the fact that Ark had something useful to add. "This topic is unrelated to today's topics, but I suppose we have time to discuss the three races. Okay, everyone, in our world, there exist three main races: the rabbits, the moles, and the sylvinites. You already know rabbits and moles, but sylvinites live in the trees. They are the most intelligent of all three races and fast, almost as fast as rabbits. They are also skilled magic users and excellent archers. They are also tall, skinny, and have egos and attitudes taller than the trees they live in."

"Wow, they sound like a bunch of jerks," said Ark.

"They are," agreed Mr. Wins. "As moles, we despise them, and they despise us. Okay, now, moving on. Er, where were we?"

"You were talking about vitality and were about to move on," said a mole in the front.

"Ah, yes, thank you. Next, we have dexterity or DEX. Rabbits also have higher-level skills for this. The difference between this and AGI is that dexterity represents how fast you can fire a bow, swing a sword, or throw a dagger, while AGI is more like actual speed in walking, running, etc. Some classes benefit heavily from DEX and AGI."

"What's a class?" asked a female mole in the front.

"That's our next topic, but we will take a break for now. Feel free to roam around the city. We meet in 2 hours." The whole class began to disperse through the door, which seemed to be stone-carved. Ark started to make his way out, and once he went outside, he was expecting to see sunlight. Then, he was reminded that they were underground.

"I mean, it's impressive and safe that this is all built underground, but I miss the sun," Ark said. "Hmm, I wonder where Arvaan is." But Ark's question was answered when he saw Arvaan waving at him from some shop.

"Arvaan!" yelled Ark.

"Where have you been, man?" said Arvaan to Ark.

"The mayor talked to me about defeating the captain, and he took me to his home. Then, the next day, I went back to school," said Ark.

Arvaan gawked at him. "You met with the mayor?! Yes, dude, that's incredible. You earned yourself a reputation, but all I ever wanted was carrots. Not to be a hero."

Arvaan shrugged. "That's just the way the wind blows. Anyway, why are you waiting at this shop here?" said Ark, looking at the incredibly lengthy line.

"It's a restaurant," said Arvaan. "I've been waiting for hours." Arvaan said as he leaned in close to Ark. "Speaking of restaurants—"

"Hours? Shhh," said Arvaan. "Please don't make a scene, but I agree this is outrageous."

"This better be good then," replied Ark. Waiting went on until they finally reached the front, where they saw a server assigning tables.

"Hi, how may I help you?" asked the server.

"We would like a table for two," Ark asked.

"All right, show your card for the reservation." Arvaan looked at Ark and then back at the server.

"I need a card to eat here?"

"Yes, you need a reservation card," she said while wiping a table.

"Err, I don't have one," said Ark.

"Then you must go to that line," the server pointed to another server. Ark looked at the line the server was pointing at, which was at least three times as long as the line they were in.

"Aw man," said Ark. "Looks like we have to go to the back of the line," said Arvaan.

"No," Ark said sadly.

"Come on, Ark, let's go." The server suddenly dropped a plate full of food.

"Wait, you're Ark," said the server, pointing the finger at Ark, "as in Ark, the captain crusher?"

"I didn't know that's what they call me these days, but yes, I defeated the captain of the raiding party."

"OMG, having you in my shop is such an honor. Let me take you to the VIP area. You don't have to worry about the line. Come on." So Ark and Arvaan followed the server to this tiny enclosed room with many blue flashing lights.

"This room is cool," said Arvaan to Ark, but Ark was too distracted by the place's majesty, many rocky areas, and blue lights.

"This is your table," said the server. "I will be serving you. My name is Isabella." After giving the pair a menu, she walked away to attend to everyone else. Ark flipped through the menu until he saw this:

"HOLY COW, 50 ALLOS FOR A BOWL OF SOUP!" Ark was lucky no one else was in the room to hear him, but Arvaan showed Ark's same concern.

"This place is expensive. What do we order?" asked Arvaan.

"We order what we can afford. How much Allos do you have on you?"

"30," said Arvaan.

"I have 20," said Ark. "We can afford one soup to share between us in two bowls."

"Okay," said Arvaan. So when Isabella returned, she asked, "What would you two like to order?"

"One soup," replied Ark.

"Are you sure? We have so much better than just soup here."

"It's all we can afford," said Ark, shrugging.

"Oh, that's why you won't order anything more. Don't worry about it. You just eating here will boost our reputation so much that the cost won't matter. Eat for free," she replied. "My boss won't care as long as you're eating."

"Oh, thanks so much, Isabella," said Ark.

"It's fine," she replied. Now, here's your menu back. I'll give you some time to think about your real menu," she said, then walked away.

"Okay, we order the most expensive thing on the menu since we're eating free."

"Nah, we shouldn't take advantage of her like that."

"But she already said our reputation boost would be enough to pay for it."

"Well, go ahead then. I'm going to order something cheaper."

Ark scrolled through the menu. Then Isabella came by.

"If you're struggling to choose, I recommend the poutine. We are famous for poutine," said Isabella.

"What's poutine?" asked Ark.

"It's fries with gravy and cheese. It tastes excellent," assured Isabella.

"Hmm, okay," said Ark, and then Isabella left.

"Ugh, Ark, why must you be such a spoilsport? Now I feel guilty for trying to order the most expensive item."

Ark chuckled. "You probably wouldn't even like the dish anyway."

"You're right; I wouldn't. It's caviar," said Arvaan. "Caviar's taste is acquired, I hear. I guess I'll order poutine, too," said Arvaan sadly.

"Cheer up. These people are famous for their poutine." A few minutes later, Isabella came by and took their order.

"So, two poutines, will that be all? We also make great Lamingtons."

"Then we'll take two of those too," replied Arvaan and Ark confidently.

"What's a Lamington?" Arvaan and Ark asked at once. Isabella laughed.

"You two boys remind me of my brothers, always getting into things they don't understand. Anyway, a Lamington is like a cake with a thin mixture of coconut. It is delicious."

"Okay, then what we said before," answered Ark.

"All right, your order will be here shortly." Then Ark and Arvaan waited. They looked outside the window and saw a colossal mining operation. They were looking for resources.

"Wow, this is a massive mine," said Arvaan.

"Indeed," agreed Ark. "Even at home, they didn't have these gigantic mines, only tiny ones."

"Speaking of which, how far are we on finding a transportation method?" asked Arvaan.

"Good. I've managed to book an appointment with Daniel Zorko."

"Nice," replied Arvaan. "We can get a method of transportation in no time."

"Mhm," agreed Ark, "but we need something faster to get us to carrot.co. I'm hoping Daniel can give us the solution."

"Yup, I agree," said Arvaan. "The mayor also sent someone to give me a letter earlier. We must sign a contract to work here and enroll as a soldier. In exchange, the city will provide us with a place to sleep and a salary of 15 allos per hour."

"Wow, that's pretty good," said Ark.

"And there's more. If we agree to this contract, we must stay here until we reach level 10. We then can move on to the next city."

"I see," said Ark, "so we need to do a lot of fighting to gain those levels."

"Indeed," replied Arvaan. "So you are finally starting to learn how the world works; better late than never," Ark said, and the two laughed together.

The order of two poutines shortly arrived after, and Ark was starving.

"This looks tasty," assured Arvaan, who had already taken his first bite, so Ark grabbed one of the fries and ate one. It was one of the most delicious things Ark had ever eaten.

"What do you think?" said Arvaan, and the only thing Ark could make out was, "Wow, it's so cheesy, and the gravy is so tasty. This is by far the second-best thing I've ever eaten."

"What's the first?" asked Arvaan.

"Carrots and it always will be." Soon after they finished the delicious poutine meal, Isabella arrived with the Lamington.

"Thanks, Isabella," said Ark.

"You're welcome," she said. Then she asked, "How was the poutine?"

"Amazing," Ark replied.

"I just knew you'd like it," she said with a smirk as she walked away. Then Ark looked at the Lamington. It looked just like a regular cake, except tiny. So Ark and Arvaan both took little pieces of the cake and downed it at the same time.

"Mmm," said Ark, "it's nice and mellow with a hint of coconut and chocolate. Good, but not as good as the poutine."

Arvaan also thought the same. The poutine was better, but the Lamington was still better than anything else at Bunny Town. Isabella came back to collect the dishes and the bill.

"Um, wait, we don't have to pay this, right?" said Ark.

"Ha-ha, of course not. It's just for you to look at how much it would cost," replied Isabella before walking off. Ark looked at the bill.

"340 allos, that's a lot," said Ark.

"Indeed," replied Arvaan. "We should tip Isabella for good service and for introducing us to poutine. That alone is worth 10,000 allos," he said.

Arvaan, Ark did not hesitate to agree. "Maybe we will tip her 10,000 allos one day," said Ark.

"One day," they both agreed.

To start, they tipped her their current savings, which was 50 allos.

"Thanks for the tips," replied Isabella.

"It's no problem," replied Ark and Arvaan. "We plan to pay you 10,000 allos for the poutine."

The waitress laughed. "Oh sure, you will," she said, then walked away. Ark left the restaurant and looked at his watch.

"An hour and thirty minutes of my time was up. Aw man, only half an hour left. What do we do?" asked Ark.

"We should sign that contract," said Arvaan.

"Yeah, right. We need to sign that for the free stay," said Ark. "Where do we go to sign it?"

"Captain Arthur's office," replied Arvaan. "We will report directly to him," Arvaan said, looking at the letter.

"All right, then let's go." The two wandered to the aboveground barracks, taking the big elevator. They then made it to a lovely rocky building the size to fit one person, and on the front, in gold letters, it said CAPTAIN ARTHUR'S OFFICE.

"It looks like we found the place," Ark said to Arvaan. They tried to open the door, but it was locked. "What do we do now?" Ark asked.

"I think we wait," replied Arvaan. They waited for fifteen minutes, and nothing happened. Then they saw a soldier, presumably a lower-ranked one, pass by and look at them.

"Um, dude, you lost or something?" said the soldier.

"We are waiting to get into Captain Arthur's office," said Arvaan.

"You have to use the side door," said the soldier as he ran off to do drills.

"Was there a side door this entire time?!" Yelled Ark. Ark and Arvaan entered through the side door, and there, in the office chair, sat Captain Arthur. On his desk, there was a massive pile of papers. He was in full beefy armor like Ark had seen during the battle, and his weapon sat on a pedestal to the side of his desk, its glory a diamond-studded iron hammer with razor-sharp spikes. Both Ark and Arvaan looked at its glory. Arthur, however, was buried in his giant stack of papers. Ark and Arvaan went to his desk and saw him looking up from his desk. Arthur saw them.

"Ah, you two boys did a great job defeating the captain. Ark, I'm impressed. I also assume you're here for the contract." He pulled a paper off his massive stack. "Sign here, and you will be enrolled in the military, starting as a private, which is what I would usually say. Except you two have performed admirably on the battlefield. Had it my way, you would both be sergeants, but with all that's happening, the best thing I can do is start you off as a corporal, one rank higher than a private. I know you two can handle the job, and you particularly could work for the elite guards," he said, pointing at Arvaan. "But the problem is our colonel is extremely picky about the people who get into the rank of sergeant or higher, so I would need his consent. My word alone won't convince him, so I hope you understand."

"It's fine," Ark and Arvaan replied, overwhelmed with the information.

"As corporals, the pay starts at 25 allos per hour, as opposed to a private who only makes 15 allos per hour. You will have to do basic responsibilities like patrolling and even transporting caravans. Now sign here," he said, giving them the paper. Ark and Arvaan signed.

"Congratulations, you both are now corporals. Any questions?" asked Arthur.

"Um, yes," said Arvaan. "You said I could make a good elite guard earlier. What's an elite guard?"

"Oh, how rude of me. Allow me to explain: the elite guards are a special division of guards that are the best of the best. Their training is so intense most die in training. The elite guards take on missions no one else would have, so many do not return alive. However, I think you will manage to take on this task and perform admirably without death," Arthur assured.

"Wow, I can't thank you enough for this opportunity," said Arvaan. Then Arthur let out a bellowing laugh.

"Not now, sonny, when you get older!"

"Oh," said Arvaan, slightly disappointed.

"Well, make yourself useful. Do 60 pushups, maggots." Then the two at once began pumping pushups: 1...2...3...4...5. This continued until 23 when Ark collapsed, and then shortly after, at 40, Arvaan collapsed.

"I can't do it," said Ark, wheezing. They were in puddles of sweat, and their arms felt dead.

"Aye, I'm impressed you did that many pushups, lads. Take a break. And you, Ark, your school's about to start. You'll only make it if you run," Arthur said teasingly. However, Ark could have spent more time. He darted off, nearly blowing the door off its hinges.

That rabbit sure is fast, said Arthur to himself as Arvaan followed closely behind. As Arvaan ran through the city, they saw the fancy restaurant they had eaten at, the barracks, and ran past the mayor's office. Ark finally made it to the school. Arvaan was nowhere to be seen because he had guard duty from signing the form. Panting and gasping from the pushups and the running, Ark burst through the school door to find Mr. Wins.

"Why, hello there, Ark. Was the break good?" he asked.

"Great," Ark said, still panting. "I got to eat poutine for the first time, and it's one of the best things I've ever eaten."

"I'm glad to hear that, Ark." As he said this, everyone began to arrive from what seemed to be a lunch break. "Okay, let's begin," Mr. Winston said as everyone settled down. "Err, where were we?"

"You were going to tell us about classes," said a mole in the front.

"Ah, right," said Mr. Winston, slapping his forehead. "So I've already told you about levels and stats, but here's the juicy part: classes are potent roles you can take on, making you powerful in certain areas, so let's get started. There are four different branches of classes: the warrior branch, the rogue branch, the archer branch, and the mage branch. These are all that higher-level people like to call base classes."

Rogue class? Isn't that the class Captain Mila was? Thought Ark to himself.

"So, let's start with the warrior branch. They specialize in damage and defense, usually at short range. We have three tiers for each class. Each tier is an upgrade of the original class, and once you reach your first tier, you will feel significantly stronger. So, the first tier one class for the warrior branch is a knight. Knights have high defense and less high offensive capabilities, typically stationed on the front lines. The second class for the warrior branch is a fencer. Unlike the knight, fencers specialize in high speed and damage over defense. They are one of the strongest classes to go up against. They wield long. Lightweight swords called rapiers that deal bleed DOTS, a damage-over-time effect. The next class is a barbarian. Like the fencer, these beasts wear little to no armor, plowing down all enemies with sheer strength. However, unlike the fencer, they have no bleed DOTS. Next, we have a combination of classes. If you pick up a weapon and gain exp with it, you will become the class related to it. For example, someone who uses a sword will become a swordsman or swordswoman. Same for other tools, each having their tiers, strengths, and weaknesses."

"Wow, there's so much versatility in classes," said Ark.

"And we aren't even close to done yet," said Winston.

"However, with that covered, I will let you learn the rest by yourself tomorrow and unlock your class."

"Wait, Winston, how do you choose a class?" asked a mole in the front.

"Oh, pardon me, I'm so silly. You choose a class by going into a class chamber. Most cities have one, including ours."

Everyone got up and began to make a run for the chamber.

"BUT WAIT," said Winston. "IT TAKES EXP TO GET A TIER 1 CLASS." Everyone skidded to a halt. "ALSO, IT TAKES A LOT OF THINKING TO PICK YOUR CLASS," he yelled. Everyone came running back.

"NO, NO, CLASS IS DISMISSED. GO DO YOUR GUARD DUTIES," shouted Winston. Ark ran to Captain Arthur's office. Exiting the elevator, he saw that it was evening and the beautiful sun was there. Ark used the side door and came in.

Arthur's office was much cleaner than before, but the mountain of paperwork remained. Burrowed in the paperwork, Arthur noticed Ark.

"Ah, you're back already," he said enthusiastically.

"School's dismissed," Ark said, panting from the running. "So, I assume you have learned what a class is then?"

"Yes," said Ark. "However, I only know a few and need clarification about what to choose."

"Hmm," Arthur stroked his chin. "You have a lot of speed, so you should select a class that benefits from high speed. You'd be fine as a rogue," Arthur said. After thinking briefly and seeing Ark's quizzical look, he quickly added, "A rogue specializes in high speed. It's more of a utility class, and its specialty is sneaking up behind people."

Exciting, thought Ark.

"BUT ENOUGH DILLY-DALLYING," said Arthur, returning to his strict self. "I have an assignment for you, Ark. It's a patrolling assignment. Recently, we have been getting strange reports of shadowy figures outside our walls. Presumably, the iron tyrant is going to attack us again. Hence, we need you to patrol outside and see if there are any threats. If there are, engage the enemy." Arthur looked at Ark's worried face. "Don't worry, Ark. We have archers who will blast the enemy with a torrent of arrows if spotted, as well as other patrol teams. You won't be going alone." Ark's face turned from worried to happy very quickly. "And don't choose Arvaan.

He's on a scouting mission. However, you will be going with my lieutenant, Sawyer. He is well-trained and robust. Good luck on your mission, Ark."

7 PATROL

Ark quickly exited the room and approached the wall; however, a security guard was there.

"Hey, um, could you open the gate, dude? I need to patrol the wall."

"No can do, sir. There are no visitors allowed outside the wall after sundown."

"But I'm a guard. I work here."

"Sorry, sir. It's strict orders from the lieutenant—"

Then suddenly, a mole slightly shorter than Arthur came into Ark's view. He had an axe on his back.

"I think I'll take it from here," he said to Ark. "Lan, I need you to open the gate."

"What is it?" Lan said, clearly frustrated until he saw who it was. "Oh, sorry, sir," he said, standing up straight, shoulders square.

"It's alright, Lan, but don't give our new corporal a hard time."

"Sorry, sir," he said, apologizing to Ark.

"Well then, we have to do guard duty," the man said to Ark.

"So you must be Arthur's lieutenant," said Ark.

"Sawyer," replied the lieutenant.

The worker mole quickly lifted the gate, so Ark and Sawyer walked out into the night. They patrolled the walls for about an hour until Sawyer spotted something.

"Ark, in the bushes!" he yelled.

Ark backed away, wielding the sword from the weapon's chest, and then a wolf stepped out of the bush. Ark wiped his brow.

"That could have been worse."

However, Sawyer charged at the wolf.

"IT'S A SCOUTING WOLF, ARK! GET HIM!"

Brandishing his axe, he missed and shook the tree in front of him down; then, a soldier fell to the ground from the tree. He quickly got up, saw Ark and Sawyer, and ran for it. Sensing he couldn't catch him, Sawyer called to the archers.

"ARCHERS, WE HAVE A THREAT DOWN HERE!"

"On it," replied one of the archers. He fired an arrow at the soldier and hit perfectly in the leg.

"Argh!" cried the enemy.

Ark got in close and slashed the soldier's leg. The soldier was disabled and could hardly move. Sawyer got in close and grabbed the soldier by his light armor.

"WHO DO YOU WORK FOR?" he loudly said.

"The Iron Tyrant," he managed to say.

"Come on, let's take him to jail," Sawyer said to Ark.

Suddenly, another soldier came into view. An archer saw that and fired an arrow, hitting the soldier's chest. Sawyer, seeing this, started to worry.

"I have a bad feeling about this."

Then, suddenly, three more soldiers came into view.

"Oh no," he said. "Ark, RUN!" said Sawyer.

The archers of Stone Haven wasted no time. As Ark and Sawyer ran, they fired a constant barrage of arrows until the enemies turned to dust. Ark and Sawyer were panting.

"Wow, that was unexpected," said Ark.

"Indeed," replied Sawyer. "The rumors are true. The Iron Tyrant's armies are still alive and well. We hardly made a dent in their numbers on that last raid."

"Oh, and our shift's over," said Ark, looking at his watch.

"Well," replied Sawyer.

"WHAT?!" said Captain Arthur, outraged at the news. After their shift was over, Ark and Sawyer went to Arthur's office.

"It's true, sir. I can confirm, and the archers, too."

Arthur stroked his chin. "I did not think it necessary, but multiply patrols around the wall and close the gate for visitors. We are on high alert."

"Understood, sir. We need to ask any nearby cities for aid. We are recovering from the last attack, and they are mounting another attack force."

"Yes, sir!" Sawyer quickly exited the room and informed

everyone that Stone Haven was highly alert. "And you, Ark, you need to go to the laboratory. Daniel will be there so you can talk to him. He informed me earlier," Arthur added, looking at Ark's face. "WELL, WHAT ARE YOU WAITING FOR? SCRAM!"

Ark ran out of the office as fast as he could. Only after running for a minute did he realize he had no idea where the lab was. So Ark skidded to a halt and went to the mayor's office, knowing the mayor probably knew where the lab was. He made it to the same furnished earthy house the mayor had loved. Going past all the paintings, Ark found the mayor working on his mountain of papers. He looked up and saw Ark.

"Hello there, Ark. How was school today? Never mind, where's the lab?" Ark responded hastily.

The mayor chuckled. "Go straight from my house and take a right, and you'll see a giant building made of stone. You can't miss it."

Ark darted out of the room and the door. He ran a bit more and found a giant stone building with a sign saying "lab"; however, the "L" had tilted slightly. Ark knocked on the door and heard a voice.

"Coming!"

Ark heard loud hammering and sawing noises, and it reeked of burnt wood. Ark covered his nose, and his ears drooped a bit. Then, a tiny mole came out.

"Daniel will be here shortly, sir; we have been informed of your arrival." Then the mole went back inside, gesturing Ark to come in.

Ark came in, the wood smell amplifying 1000 times, and the sawing getting louder. The sight was incredible: cannons everywhere.

"Woah," said Ark.

"Yes, it's all awe-inspiring," said the mole hurriedly. He dragged Ark's arm to the other side. Ark saw a wall.

"What's here? It's just a wall."

"That's what it looks like to commoners; however, to scientists," he said, placing a hand on the wall, "it's different."

Suddenly, the wall moved to the side, revealing a door. Ark was gawking at the door.

"Wah-wah-what?" said Ark, dumbfounded, while the mole looked at the wall happily.

"This was all my work, you know? But that's not important," he said, fitting a key into the door lock.

The door opened, and Ark and the mole walked inside. They saw an office piled with papers and a mini area for science work. Daniel worked on a project with something in his ears.

"Daniel!" shouted the tiny mole exasperatedly.

Daniel continued to work but didn't hear anything.

"DANIEL!!" yelled the mole so loud that Ark clutched his ears in pain.

Daniel removed what Ark assumed were earbuds and looked at Ark and the mole. Then he rose off the ground and quickly shook hands with Ark.

"It's a pleasure to see you here, Ark," said Arvaan's witty friend. The tiny mole exited the office, leaving Ark and Daniel to themselves. Daniel sat at his desk, which was also piled with papers like Captain Arthur's office; however, at the back were countless awards for Scientist of the Year and medals for science and innovation.

"Woah," said Ark, looking at his medals.

"Earning those prizes took a long time, and I've studied for years. Anyway, to the point, what do you want?"

"I need a mode of transportation to get me to Carrot.co," he said, pointing to a map conveniently on Daniel's desk.

"Interesting. I assume, to get that far, horses are out of the question," said Daniel, stroking his chin.

"Even really fast horses?" asked Ark.

"Forget that. It can only get you to Carrot.co. Also, I'm not sure if you're aware, but the Iron Tyrant has captured Carrot.co. He's using it to feed his soldiers. However, in a city with a higher ranking than here, I know a few friends willing to try to attack Carrot.co and take it back. There's a lot of discussion in higher-level rabbit cities because, as you know, your kind couldn't go a day without carrots, no offense."

"None taken," replied Ark, "but they still require a transportation method," added Ark.

"Indeed," replied the mole. "They have some vortex mages to help them get there, though."

"What's a vortex mage?" asked Ark, confused.

8 THE PACKAGE

A vortex mage is a class in the mage branch that allows mages to create vortexes looking at Ark's face. Daniel added, "Vortexes are portals that can instantly take you from one place to another."

"WHAT?!" yelled Ark. "Why didn't we use that before?!"

"Let me finish next time," said Daniel, shaking his head disapprovingly. "First, vortexes are a trade secret that only the rabbits know. Second, the capital for vortex mage training lives right next to us, not too far away, maybe like a 2-hour ride with a horse. However, Captain Arthur doesn't like the Mayor who leads that city, and they have tensions. And finally, there are limitations to vortexes. How far you can stretch them depends on how good you are at magic, and it's hard to come by people who are good at it and willing to help you."

"But wait," Captain Arthur said, "we needed immediate aid from someone to prepare for another attack."

"So what?" said Daniel, annoyed. "We could knock two birds with one stone. If we repair relations with the Mayor there, we can secure transport to Carrot.co and gain their aid if an assault occurs."

For once, Daniel didn't know what to say. Then he stroked his beard and paced over the office. After a few minutes, he finally said, "We need to contact the mayor as soon as possible." He clicked a button on his desk and spoke into a microphone. "I need a scientist to contact the Mayor and bring him to my office."

Five minutes later, the Mayor came running into the office. "Okay, Mr. Mayor, I have a proper—"

"It's fine, Daniel; your scientist told me the details."

"Ah, okay. What's your opinion on this?" He eagerly awaited the Mayor's response.

"We need to gather the council's opinion on this. That includes Arthur, you, me, and the elders."

"Understood, sir."

"What about me, Sir?" asked Ark.

"You can come too because you suggested this plan."

"Actually," Daniel interjected, "I informed him mostly about the plan, so I deserve the credit." Ark and the Mayor just looked at Daniel. "What? I did inform him."

Ark looked at the Mayor, then Daniel, and just laughed.

While laughing, the Mayor ran out of the room to fetch his assistants to round up the council.

About an hour later, one of the Mayor's assistants came to the lab to fetch Ark for the council.

"Oh no," he said, looking at Ark's clothes. "This will not do."

"What?"

"Why not?" said Ark, looking down at his leather clothes that he usually put on.

"You need formal clothing for this," said the Mayor's assistant. "Come on, let me take you to the suit store."

So together, Andrew (the Mayor's assistant) and Ark went to the gigantic suit building.

"Woah," said Ark, looking at the building. "There's nothing but surprises here in Stone Haven."

He walked into the building and saw moles everywhere, buying different clothes. They all stared at Ark.

"Um, why is everyone looking at me?" he whispered, asking Andrew.

He whispered back, "Because you're the only rabbit here and because you're the Captain Crusher."

They wandered around with every mole in the shop, staring at Ark. To him, it felt like the room had suddenly gotten hotter, and then a mole with his suit came up to Ark and shook his hand.

"Well, if it isn't the Captain Crusher. Welcome to my suit store; I assume you're looking for a suit."

"Indeed," replied Andrew, cutting Ark off as he was about to say something. "We are looking for a suit that would fit Ark."

"Then come with me. We have just the thing for you." Ark and Andrew followed the owner to the back aisle.

Just then, Ark began to notice the prices. Some were in the 50s, others in the thousands, but what surprised Ark the most was a suit on display in a fancy stand and the price tag: 10,000 Allos.

"O...M...G, that's expensive," the owner noticed his look and explained why it was so expensive. This was a one-of-a-kind shirt we got from a master tailor. However, he died recently. Look closely, Ark, at the lapels. It was trimmed with diamonds and Aerolite." Ark was about to ask what Aerolite was, but the owner dragged him to look at a suit.

It was a regular black suit with a red tie. "Looks like the average suit," said Ark, unimpressed.

"Well, looks can be deceiving," said the manager. He unfurled the suit and showed Ark the inside. It was fully lined with iron armor.

"Woah," said Ark, now impressed. The manager gave the suit to Ark; he tried it on and came out of the dressing room. It was a perfect fit, and as a side bonus, it provided protection.

"You look good, Ark," said Andrew, impressed. Now, let's go to the council table in the city hall."

Ark and Andrew made it to the city hall. Like the Mayor's house, it had marble pillars and stone walls, giving it an earthy feeling. They arrived inside, and Ark immediately noticed how nice it was: red carpets, stone walls, a chandelier, and a massive gold table.

Ark took a seat; everyone else had already arrived, even

Arvaan.

"Okay," said the Mayor. Let's start. We know that an attack is imminent. They want to destroy higher-ranking cities' food supply by taking us out. Arthur, can you confirm that an attack is imminent?"

"Yes, Sir," responded Arthur. "My troops have seen scout wolves and teams patrolling our walls, likely looking for a weak point."

"Understood," replied the Mayor. "Send a construction team to ensure our walls are in tip-top shape."

"Yes, sir," replied someone who Ark assumed to be the building foreman. "The next thing we must do is ask a city for aid if an attack befalls us," continued the Mayor, "and the nearest one to us, as Daniel and Ark proposed, is Vortex City. They could send aid with their vortexes in the blink of an eye."

"Oh, no way," said a voice. Ark turned to see who it was; it was Arthur. "That Mayor is a bloody idiot with her stupid cheese-rolling competitions and terrible leadership."

"Arthur, be reasonable," said the Mayor. "It's the safest option to gain their aid so they could support us quickly," the Mayor pleaded.

"Nope," said Arthur, rolling his eyes. Then Arvaan spoke up. "Even if we could get Captain Arthur's approval, how would we convince them to help us?"

"That's where the next part of my plan comes into play,"

said the Mayor. We give them our great armor and weaponry, and they will surely side with us despite our racial differences. We have worked with rabbits before."

"How do we have such great weaponry?" asked Ark. "Because moles are naturally better at mining, harvesting, and crafting armor than rabbits, and we have plenty of armor to spare."

"And if they don't accept?" said one of the elders. "Then we give them this." He pulled out a grubby little package no larger than a pencil case. All the elders and Captain Arthur gasped.

"Are you sure, Sir?" Captain Arthur said, flabbergasted. That package is precious. What's in it?" Ark asked, barely staying in his seat.

"A bargaining chip of immense power," said the Mayor. "Unfortunately, if I told you exactly what it is, I would be obliged to kill you."

"Oh, my," said Ark, no longer excited. "If we know that we can get Vortex City's help, we will be able to win the battle."

"Then we best get moving," said the Mayor. "There was some murmuring among the elders and Captain Arthur. I still say no," Ark heard Arthur say. "If we give our armor and weapons and the package, they likely will make this a one-time deal, as in we give up the package for their aid temporarily."

"Agreed," said one of the elders. However, an army is on the way, and we can't handle it. We did it last time, but only because of the cannon," Elder Grey decided to speak up. That's it; we need to gain Vortex City's alliance now. No more waiting."

Arthur was about to protest until another mole came darting in. He had dirty maps in his hands that showed years of wear and unorganized notes and a compass on his helmet; by looks, he was a scout. "Sir, our scouts have picked up their army; it's about 8 hours away from the destination if we are lucky." The council members exchanged worried glances; even Arthur looked taken aback.

Now visibly worried, the Mayor asked, "How big is their army?"

The scout's face went pale. "If the last fight we fought was considered an army, consider these five armies. They are all armored to the teeth, and their commander looks a lot like a very high-ranking officer."

"Oh, my," said the Mayor. Captain Arthur, who was usually calm, did not protest and looked worried.

"Now, I suppose there's no need for a vote," said the Mayor. "Arthur, schedule a convoy; we need Vortex City's aid immediately."

The council had disbanded, and Ark reported to Captain Arthur with Arvaan. They used the side door, and Arthur's desk was no longer stacked with papers but with his backup sword, which he was sharpening. He looked up and saw the two. "Sit down," he said. The two grabbed a seat and listened.

"We need a convoy," he said, "and I've chosen you two to

be that convoy."

9 TRANSPORT

"Us?" said Ark and Arvaan at the same time.

"Indeed, my top moles barely beat you in speed. You two have speed moles that you can't acquire so easily. And on your convoy, take this with you." Arthur pulled out the exact package Ark had seen before. It was a very tiny package. Ark took it, but Arthur held on and whispered in his ear, "Lose this, and the Mayor will have my head on a wall."

"Woah," said Ark, "that serious, huh?"

"Extremely. And whatever you do, don't open that package." The curiosity was killing Ark, but he ignored Arthur's wish. "Here are the details," Arthur said. "I will give you the fastest horses we own and the caravan. Also, here are some potions." He handed Ark a few glowing green bottles of substance. "They're all weak strength and speed potions, but weak is better than none. Next, you will be meeting Sawyer at the stable. He will give you the caravan and the horses. Once you have those, depart for Vortex City, and Sawyer will give you a map."

Ark rushed to the stable (Arthur had told him where it was), and when he arrived, he saw Arvaan and gave him a complicated handshake. Soon after, Sawyer arrived.

"Here's the map, Ark," he said, handing Ark the map.

"I will do my best to get there."

"Atta boy," said Sawyer, painfully patting him on the back. Ark climbed onto his horse and hitched the wagon with armor to it. Arvaan fed the horse an apple. The horse neighed happily, and Ark was about to depart when he saw a mole running towards him.

"WAIT!" the mole yelled. Ark skidded his horse to a halt and climbed off to see who it was. It was Daniel, and he was panting.

"W-wait. I have something for you, Ark." He pulled out a metal disk with a red button in the middle the size of a carrot pie and gave it to Ark. "When all seems lost, put this on your chest and hit the button."

"Okay?" said Ark, confused. "What does it do?"

"Let's just say it will give you an edge in battle. We don't have time to waste. Be wary of thieves along the path, and good luck," said Daniel. But Ark's horse had taken off in a flash before he finished. Daniel laughed to himself. "What am I worried about? They'll be fine.....I hope."

2 Hours Later

"That's like the third poster I've seen," said Arvaan.

"The third poster for what?" asked Ark.

"The third poster for these hoodlums without hoods called the Deadly Tea Leaf Brothers." Then Arvaan saw another poster and quickly grabbed it off a tree to show Ark. "The Deadly Tea Leaf Brothers."

Ark read, "Wanted for 50,000 Allos dead or alive. Crimes include robbing Vortex City, tax evasion, second-degree murder, first-degree murder, armed robbery, stealing secure Lunaria cargo, the looting of treasuries..." The crimes went on.

"Woah," said Ark, "no wonder they want these guys behind bars."

"Agreed," said Arvaan, tossing the paper as it whizzed off. If Ark had to guess, they traveled about ten times as fast as his regular running.

"It's nice that they gave us this horse," he said.

"It is," agreed Arvaan. They continued at blazing speed until an arrow whizzed by Ark's head.

"What was that for?!"

Then their horse tripped on some goo, and the two of them went flying. "AHHHH!" They crashed into a tree. Ark got up as fast as he could.

"Who's there?!"

He heard chuckling in the background and saw two figures emerging from the shadows, one significantly larger than the other wielding a giant sword, the other smaller wielding a crossbow and a quiver of arrows.

"WE ARE THE DEADLY TEA LEAF BROTHERS!" the larger one boomed.

"No...." said Ark and Arvaan together.

"AND WE HAVE COME TO ROB YOUR PATHETIC CARAVAN!" said the bigger one as the smaller one dug through the wagon.

"Ooh, nice armor and swords. All molevern-made. This loot will fetch a great price," he said to himself. Arvaan stood up and charged at the larger brother with the hammer he had acquired from the weapon's chest. The larger brother easily deflected, hitting him with the flat side of his sword and sending him flying into a tree.

"ARVAAN!" yelled Ark.

"What is wrong with you?" said the larger brother. "We haven't even introduced ourselves, and you are going to pick a fight?! Didn't your mother ever teach you manners?"

"Umm, what?" Ark said, taken aback. You attacked us first," Ark countered.

"Oh well, he has a point," said the larger brother to the more minor brother.

"My bad, bro," responded the more minor brother.

"Okay, are you ready for this brother?"

"Positively"

"I'm Kian and he's Destry" said Kian the bigger brother pointing to Destry the smaller brother.

Arvaan had climbed out of the tree and ran to Ark

"They're both rabbits, so we should expect them to be fast, more than strong," whispered Arvaan.

"I don't know," said Ark, "Kian looks menacing with that massive sword of his."

"Hmmm," thought Arvaan. "What if we-"

"Wait," said Kian, rubbing his eyes. "Destry, that looks like that chap who took out Captain Mila. Isn't that funny?"

Destry squinted, pulled out a piece of paper, and compared the paper to Ark. "No brother, he IS the chap who took out Captain Mila."

"Oh my," replied Kian. "We best take them out fast. We have our match worth against them," said Destry.

"Oh, finally," said Kian, banging his fists together. "I've been itching for a fight."

Ark gulped and drew his sword. "Well, if it's a fight you want, then it's a fight you will get!" Ark dashed at Kian. Destry fired an arrow at Ark, which got him right in the knee.

"Ugh," said Ark, slowing down. However, while Ark was distracting them, Arvaan snuck behind them.

"SURPRISE!" he said as he slammed down his hammer. When the dust cleared, no one was hurt. Kian used his sword to block and hit Arvaan back to where Ark was.

"They are tough, and our fighting skills are terrible," said Arvaan.

Ark hated to admit it, but it was true. They had had little to no fighting experience. Ark and Arvaan charged at the two together. They were met with two arrows and a sword to the face. They went flying again.

"This is absurd," said Ark. "We have hardly made a dent in their armor."

"NOW IT'S TIME WE TAKE THE OFFENSIVE! CHARGE!" Ark had barely gotten up when Kian slashed his sword at him. Ark dodged by using his hands to move his massive sword, but not completely. It sliced his shoulder.

"Ugh, so much pain," said Ark. He couldn't go on much longer like this; he wasn't faring well. As for Arvaan, Destry kept shooting arrows at him. There were at least twenty arrows in his body if Ark had to guess. They were both worn out.

"Had enough?" replied Kian with a smug face.

"Just warming up," said Ark, trying not to show weakness. Ark was wondering if he should surrender just for Arvaan's sake, but then he remembered all the people that would be massacred if he didn't go to Vortex City. The army would lay waste to Stonehaven, leaving nothing behind. Arvaan rose, seeing the determination in Ark's eyes.

"I'm ready to fight and I'm with you."

"Wow," said Destry, "these two just don't give up. Maybe we should spare them so we can use them as a punching bag."

"Too bad that won't be happening," said Ark. He remembered he had potions in his bag and pulled them out, one for Ark, one for Arvaan. He tossed the potion to Arvaan with a look that said, "Chug."

"Brother! They are using potions. We must kill them before they kill us!" shouted Destry, notching an arrow.

"At ease," said Kian, lowering Destry's weapon. "I enjoy a good challenge. Drink up," he said to Ark and Arvaan. They both drank the potions. It tasted like chalk and drywall to Ark and Arvaan, but they felt themselves growing stronger in an instant. Ark's legs felt more capable, while Arvaan's arms felt more potent than before. He swung his hammer around with ease.

Ark dashed at Kian with renewed vigor, striking him so fast it caught him off guard. Kian tried swinging his sword at him, but Ark jumped on Kian's sword and performed a downward strike with his sword. The blade clanged off the metal, with sparks flying everywhere. Then Arvaan came with his hammer and struck Kian's chest plate directly, sending him flying back and hitting a tree.

"Woah, these new powers are wicked," said Arvaan.

Destry fired an arrow at Ark, but because of his new speed, he sliced the arrow in half with his sword in midair. Destry looked at him, clearly shocked. Ark wasted no time. He dashed at him and cut his arm with his sword. Destry tried to reload an arrow, but Ark kept fighting relentlessly.

Meanwhile, Arvaan and Kian were going at it, their massive weapons colliding. Then, in desperation, Arvaan slammed his hammer on the ground. It created a mini tremor that shook

Kian. Then Arvaan slammed his hammer right at Kian's helmet. Rattling his body and starting to crush his armor.

Ark had Destry on the ground. Ark had tried to break his crossbow using his leg, but it was made of metal. He ended up hurting himself. "Ow!"

Destry laughed, but Ark quickly silenced him, putting a sword to his chin. "Alright, you win," said Destry.

"That's more like it," said Ark. Arvaan and Kian were still battling. Kian's armor was beginning to break down.

"They told me this was the best armor in Vortex City," whined Kian, more significant cracks forming.

"Haven't you heard? Not everything you hear is true."

"How are you so strong?" cried Kian, struggling to block Arvaan's hammer blows. Then Ark appeared with Arvaan. "The power of teamwork!" they said simultaneously. While Destry was left unattended, he realized Ark had taken his crossbow.

"Smart," said Destry. He thought about his secret weapon. "Is it worth it?" he said to himself. He sighed. "No choice." He wasn't the only rabbit who had potions. He pulled out a glowing red bottle. "This had better be as good as they said it was." He drank the potion, and his whole body began to shake. The taste was burning until he couldn't hold it in anymore. "AHHHHH!" His scream rang through the air. Ark and Arvaan heard Destry's horrific scream. Even Kian looked revolted.

"Oh no, don't tell me he used it," Kian muttered.

"Go, Ark! I'll deal with Kian." Ark ran over to where he had left Destry. He was unarmed as before.

"Well, hello there, Ark," said Destry, his voice now more profound than before. His stance looked more vital than before. Instead of his regular blue eyes, they were dark red now. Let us fight," he said.

Ark got into his sloppy battle stance. Destry dashed at lightning speed, much faster than he was before. He performed an uppercut with his hands, temporarily stunning Ark. Destry performed a swift kick that knocked Ark with the force of a elephant. Ark got pushed back into a tree, but Destry wasn't finished. He performed multiple punches and grabbed his crossbow from Ark's bag. Then Destry fired arrows at blazing speed. It was continuous. Ark had at least 20 arrows in his body.

"Ugh, I don't know if I can go on," said Ark.

"Had enough?" replied Destry with a wicked look.

"Only getting warmed up," said Ark. He dashed at Destry using his potion-boosted legs, but apparently, the potion Destry drank was more potent. He caught Ark's sword and threw it to the side. Then Destry began to punch him over and over again. Then he reloaded his crossbow and shot Ark another time.

"I can hardly go on," he said, crawling on the ground. Then he remembered something. He had one last weapon. Arvaan came into Ark's view. He saw that Ark was crawling on the ground.

"Ark! Are you okay?"

"F-fine," replied Ark. He could barely make out the words.

"What happened to Kian?"

"Tied up, Ark. I got him good. All his armor broke," replied Arvaan.

Then Destry decided to run at lightning speed and punched Arvaan to the floor. Now, they were both on the floor. Their legs and arms began to feel weaker.

"No," said Arvaan, "the potion's wearing off."

"Wait," said Ark. "I have one last weapon."

"You're bluffing!" said Destry, punching him more. Ark pulled out the metal disc with the button Daniel had given him. Even though everything hurt, he tried to put it on, but Destry fired an arrow at it. The disc went flying, but Arvaan caught it.

"What do I do with this, Ark?!"

"Hit the button!" he screamed. Arvaan placed the disc on his chest and hit the button. The metal began to whir, and then it started to cover Arvaan's body. He was growing more significant with the metal. It covered him entirely, and a visor came up, showing his face. He was two times larger than before, and the metal had turned into a bulky armor for Arvaan. Destry looked flabbergasted.

"Woah gang, this is cool," Arvaan's voice projected somehow. Destry screamed a battle cry and fired at least 30 arrows. All the arrows bounced off the thick armor.

"Argh," said Destry. He pulled out a red-tipped arrow. "Try this on for size!" He fired the red-tipped arrow, and there was a huge blast.

"ARVAAN!" yelled Ark.

"YES," yelled Destry, but when the smoke cleared, Destry could make out the exact bulky figure.

"Impossible!" Destry said.

Then, with a loud battle cry, Arvaan charged with his new armor, punching Destry with his metal arm. Destry blocked with his crossbow, but the punch was so fierce it bent his crossbow in half. Destry threw his crossbow to the floor and used a full power punch on Arvaan's suit. Destry felt the blowback as Arvaan stood unaffected.

"Argh!" cried Destry. He had broken his fingers trying to punch the armor. "Had enough, gangster?" said Arvaan.

"Just getting started," said Destry. Then he felt much weaker, the power draining from his arms. He gasped in shock. "No, no! NO! Not now!" He started to feel as weak as a chicken and dropped to the ground, his voice barely audible. His eyes turned back to normal. "No..."

Ark summoned the energy to get up and pulled out the handcuffs that Captain Arthur had given him. "You're under arrest," he said. Then Ark ran to Arvaan and gave him a high five.

"We did it!"

Then Arvaan pressed the same button he used to turn on his armor. The metal began to shrink back into a metal disc. "Neat tool Daniel invented. It's saved our lives," said Arvaan. Ark made a mental note to thank him later.

"Well then, how are we going to take them to Vortex City?" asked Ark.

"We just carry them on the wagon," replied Arvaan.

"That sounds harsh. "

"If the situations were reversed, Kian wouldn't think twice."

"True," said Ark. "Let's do that." Ark carried Destry to the horse. It was neighing gently after watching the fight. Ark hitched the wagon back and threw Destry onto the wagon. Meanwhile, Arvaan cuffed Kian and brought him over.

"You haven't heard the last of us! We will kill you all!"

"Sure, buddy," said Arvaan, throwing him into the wagon but noticing that there was a bag in Kian's armor. Ark, curious, pulled it out. He at once saw the bag's weight. It was cumbersome. Ark struggled to lift it; then, he laid it on the ground. He opened it, eager to see what was inside. In it, he found fish. The bag was filled to the brim with fish. Ark eyed Kian suspiciously as Kian was sweating. Arvaan came over to see what the deal was with the bag.

"Yo bro, why is this bag full of fish?" asked Arvaan, confused.

"I don't know," said Ark, equally confused.

"Do we take it with us?" asked Arvaan.

"Sure," said Ark, feeling his stomach rumble. "Pass me one," said Ark.

"Okay, bro," replied Arvaan, handing him the bag. Ark started a fire and cooked the fish on the fire. Ark pulled it off and took a bite eagerly when it looked like it was ready to eat. It was the second most delightful taste sensation Ark had ever felt, only second to carrots.

"Wow, this tastes good," said Ark, chomping the fish down.

"Try one," said Ark, reaching for the next fish. Arvaan grabbed one and ate it.

"WOW! This fish is the best fish I've ever tasted."

"I know, right?" said Ark. The two chatted over the fish, and then they eventually started back on the horse; Kian and Destry hitched on the wagon and rode off.

10 WELCOME TO VORTEX CITY

One hour later

"I SEE IT! WE FINALLY SEE IT!!!" Ark's voice echoed with a mix of awe and excitement. Vortex City, with its high walls of stone and wood braces, stood before them, a testament to rabbit ingenuity and strength. It was a sight far more impressive than Stonehaven, with its few ballistae and lack of a cannon. The fish they had consumed transformed them, making them feel faster, stronger, and somehow more intelligent.

Just as they were about to enter, a guard rabbit, dressed in spiffy clothing, approached. "Welcome to Vortex City. Now get out," he said, his voice tinged with boredom. "They've had me on welcoming duty for three days," he added, clearly exasperated. His demeanor changed, however, when he noticed the wagon and the bound Tea Leaf Brothers. "WHAT??!?" he exclaimed, his shock palpable. "You caught them..." he stammered. "GUARDS, GO FETCH THE MAYOR!" he ordered, his voice now filled with urgency. The guards scurried away, leaving Ark and Arvaan in a state of mild confusion. "Woah, he must be a high-ranking officer," Ark whispered to Arvaan.

"I'm the colonel of this fine city," said the colonel, catching the conversation. "The name's Colonel Ishaan," he said, reaching out. Ark shook his hand. "I'm Ark, and this is Arvaan." "Yo, what's good, bro," Arvaan said, shaking Ishaan's hand and giving him a fist bump.

As they were about to explain, a group of rabbits with shields emerged from the gate, surrounding a rabbit that Ark assumed was the mayor. "What's the meaning of this?" the mayor, Julia, asked Colonel Ishaan. "Sorry to interrupt you, Miss Julia. However, this needs immediate attention." The mayor examined the wagon and noticed the deadly Tea Leaf Brothers. Then Julia's gaze fell on Ark and Arvaan. "Impossible," she muttered, her eyes fixed on the bound Tea Leaf Brothers. "Who is responsible for this?" she demanded. "These two, madam," said Colonel Ishaan, pointing towards Ark and Arvaan. "No way," she said, pulling up her stat screen. "These two are a lower level than five, and the deadly Tea Leaf Brothers are level nine. These guys would get destroyed." "Yet they turned out alive, and they captured them," Colonel Ishaan pointed out. "This is how we did it," said Ark, taking the armor from Arvaan and hitting the button. The disc began to whir, and it transformed into a full metal suit with a red visor. "WOAH," Julia exclaimed, her surprise evident. "What is that?"

"Oh?" "Are you interested in it?" asked Ark, flexing his iron muscles. "Okay, now I see how you beat the deadly Tea Leaf Brothers. Come to my office," said Julia, darting off. "I'll take you guys there," said Colonel Ishaan. Ark turned off his armor as it materialized back into the disc. The three ran across the city. While running, Ark saw rabbits everywhere. "It seems this is a rabbit city," he said to Arvaan. "Indeed, it is," replied Arvaan, noticing all the rabbits. Unlike Stonehaven, most buildings were made of wood. "Reminds me of home," Ark thought to himself.

The three finally reached a big, grand building and walked inside. There was a big table like the one in the city hall of Stonehaven. Julia was sitting in a seat towards the end of the table. Colonel Ishaan took a seat, so they took a seat as well. "So, why are you two here and with a wagon full of goodies? I liked what I saw; high-quality armor and weapons were all Molevern crafted," said Julia. "Stonehaven is in trouble. A giant army bigger than anything we've seen before is coming, and they will be here soon," said Ark, feeling braver than he was.

"Interesting," said Colonel Ishaan. "Is it the Iron Tyrant's armies?" "Yes," said Arvaan. Julia spoke up instantly. "Not those troublemakers," said Julia. "They destroyed a huge city famous for potions recently. To eradicate one of their armies would bring us a lot of stature points," said Julia. "What are those?" asked Ark. "Stature points are used to represent cities.

The more you have, the more funding you get from the capital. They can be gained through situations precisely like this one," said Colonel Ishaan.

"So, I see you need aid," continued Julia. "I'm willing to help," said Julia, "for the wagon of goods, which I assume is for the aid. However, I need a little more value." Ark sighed and pulled out the package the mayor had given him. Julia somehow recognized it instantly. "Impossible," she said, mouth hanging open. "I suppose we have a deal?" asked Ark. Julia shook Ark's hand. "Yes, we do."

11 PREPARATION

Here's the deal," said Colonel Ishaan, "we don't have our vortex mages ready yet; we only have one ready enough to give you both a ticket back."

"So, vortex mages can create portals that can teleport you worldwide instantly?" asked Arvaan.

"You're mostly right. However, the Vortexes have limitations," said Colonel Ishaan. "The farther you want the portals to go, the more experienced you must be. Sometimes, you need multiple mages and portals to transport large items a short distance, and the worst part is the cooldown after using a vortex. They have cooldowns varying from hours to weeks depending on your skills."

"Our vortex mages will be ready in a few hours," said Colonel Ishaan.

"The army will be here by then," said Ark worriedly.

"You will just have to hold out," said Colonel Ishaan, his expression grim. Then, a rabbit in shining purple robes with stars and a wizard hat came into Ark's view. He seemed to be a vortex mage. "Create a vortex," instructed Colonel Ishaan. The wizard obliged and twirled his staff until a big purple circle with arcs of white lightning appeared.

"Good luck, Ark and Arvaan," said Colonel Ishaan. "Until we meet again." Colonel Ishaan shook both of their hands, and Ark and Arvaan were pushed into the portal. It was white light for them until they felt a gentle breeze on their skin. They had arrived back in Stonehaven. They saw their walls in the distance and the familiar smell of smoke and coal.

"You'd think that, for having the best vortex mages, they could have positioned it better," said Ark, running.

"It's fine, you need the exercise." They ran past the gate and to the city hall. When they nearly blew the door off its hinges, the mayor saw them aghast and welcomed them into the familiar gold table. It seemed Captain Arthur and the elders were planning a defense.

"Welcome back, Ark and Arvaan. Judging by how fast you came back, I suppose we have secured a deal," the mayor asked.

"Indeed, however, they will only arrive in a few hours. All their vortex mages are on cooldown, and regular transportation is too slow," said Arvaan.

"So, we have a holdout, eh?" said Daniel Zorko, who was also at the meeting.

"It seems that way," said the mayor.

"I have instructed all soldiers to halt training and rest for the upcoming fight. Our best blacksmiths are forging weapons as we speak," said Arthur. Ark and Arvaan took a seat at the familiar gold table.

"So, what's our plan of defense?" asked Ark.

"Like last time, we send cavalry to the frontlines, and our archers and siege weaponry will defend," said Captain Arthur.

"Will that be enough for such a huge army?" asked Lieutenant Sawyer.

"I originally doubted it, and I still don't think that this will be enough, but Daniel has six cannons ready that will surely provide us aid in battle," said Arthur.

"This battle could last for hours. We need our soldiers and walls in tip-top shape," said an elder.

"Already done, madam," said what seemed to be a building foreman.

"Alright, seeing how this is how we will approach, this meeting is now over. Enjoy the rest of your day and rest up for the fight ahead," said the mayor. Arvaan immediately rushed to Ark.

"Come on, we must get armor and weapons for the fight," he said, dragging Ark towards the shopping area. They saw an armor and weapons store called Slash and Defend Weapons Store. Arvaan dragged Ark inside. They saw a beautiful array of swords and shields, and the most remarkable set of armor

Ark had ever seen, even more incredible than Captain Arthur's armor.

"Like what you see, sonny?" asked the shopkeeper. "That be high-quality mithril armor. That won't be breaking on you for a very long time." Ark thought this was good until he saw the price tag and moved to a different area. Meanwhile, Arvaan looked at weapons, his eyes fixed on a massive two-handed spear.

"First, you want a hammer, and now a spear?" asked Ark, rolling his eyes.

"What?" said Arvaan. "I like weapons. Anyways, I wasn't thinking about buying this one," he said, moving onto the next aisle. The store was completely packed with people, mostly soldiers, preparing for the battle. Then Ark saw a weapon on a stand that caught his eye. It was like a sword. However, it looked lighter and sharper. It bore a magnificent purple hilt and a gleaming blade. No one was watching, so Ark quickly grabbed and swung with it.

"Wow, this is amazing," said Ark, effortlessly doing hundreds of slashes quickly.

"That is one of our finest blades," said the shopkeeper, seeing Ark slash it. Then, a crowd gathered around to watch Ark slash the lightweight sword.

"That is also known as a rapier, like a lighter version of a sword, easier to swing around and sharper," said the shopkeeper. Eventually, The shop owner gathered around the whole shop. Ark was moving so fluently with the sword. It was almost like a dance.

"Woah," said the shopkeeper, impressed. "Where did you learn to do that?"

Ark felt embarrassed. "It's some moves I picked up from watching others"

"Quit being so modest, mate. That's some great wielding of the rapier. You should be a fencer."

"I'd love to, but I'm not sure it's right. Can you give me a rundown?"

"The fencer is a high-risk, high-reward class. It moves fast and hits hard. However, its armor is pathetic, wearing light or no armor for experts."

"Hmm, I'll think about it," said Ark. "But even if I wanted to be a fencer, I couldn't afford this magical weapon."

The shopkeeper thought this through and put a hand on Ark's shoulder. "I will give you this for free if you promise to fight your best on the battlefield and keep my family alive."

"Yes, I'll do my best," said Ark. The shopkeeper, true to his word, gave Ark the rapier for free. Arvaan had also gotten them some armor: light armor for Ark and heavy armor for Arvaan. Then the two dashed towards the walls, surprised to see many guards waiting for the army. Ark looked at the guards' faces and noticed they were very pale.

"What's the matter with you guys?" asked Ark.

"A scout came back," said a familiar guard with an axe; it was Sawyer. "The army's merely an hour away, and it's massive. It outnumbers us two to one." Ark sensed fear in his voice; he was feeling scared. Arvaan shivered next to Ark, but it was barely noticeable due to the new armor. The other guards looked as if they had seen a ghost. Ark and Arvaan had climbed to the top of the wall and saw the horizon. The skies were getting darker, and lightning flashed in the skies, spooking the cavalry ready to disperse. There were last-minute checks on the wall and the gate. A few guards rolled up the cannons; there were six of them, all in shiny paint.

"We're ready," thought Ark to himself. "If we can't defend this place, no one can." It had been half an hour until Captain Arthur and the mayor had arrived. The mayor got on a podium and used Daniel's microphone.

"Fellow soldiers, there is lay an army on the horizon," there was a flash of lightning. "They may be strong. There will be death, pain, and suffering in that battle. I cannot guarantee all of you will return home alive, but remember why we fight. We cannot allow the iron tyrant to rule our people with dictatorship and destroy our city. We must stand united as one. We will triumph over this threat as we have triumphed over the threats before. A few days ago, there was another battle. The iron tyrant thought he could walk on in and destroy our city. Well, we showed them. I admire your bravery in walking onto that battlefield and fighting for your loved ones. WE WILL

PREVAIL AND DESTROY THEM FOR ALL OF VISCLAND!" Cheers went up in the audience. The soldiers began to look happier.

"YEAH, DOWN WITH THE IRON TYRANT!" yelled another soldier.

"Good thing he did that speech," said Daniel, who had appeared behind Ark and Arvaan.

"Yeah, good thing," said Ark. "The soldiers were starting to get worried." There were more cheers in the crowd until—

"I SEE THEM!" yelled an archer on a watchtower.

"Huh? Where?" said Ark, desperately trying to investigate the night.

"You can't see them because archer classes have better vision," said the mayor. All the color drained from the archer's face when he took another glance at the army.

"H-how i-is this p-possible?" he stammered.

"What is it?!" yelled the mayor, concerned. The archer was too dazed to reply, so Daniel smacked him with a fish.

"SOLDIER, WHAT DID YOU SEE ON THAT BATTLEFIELD?!" he commanded.

The soldier tried to make out words, but his mouth just sputtered. Then, at last, the army came into view. Each footstep taken echoed in the night. The army was colossal. It looked as though they had been destroying countless cities. Scars were etched on their cheeks, and fur singed, but Ark noticed a peculiar creature in the back despite all this. It had fiery red eyes, large scales, diamond-hard skin, and razor-sharp teeth. It was no doubt in Ark's mind that what he saw was a dragon.

"Impossible," he said, equally bewildered as the rest of the troops. "How in the world did they get a dragon? They're extinct!" said the mayor. The dragon roared at maximum strength into the night and breathed fire on an enemy soldier. "HEY, WATCH IT. YOU'RE ON OUR SIDE," said an enemy soldier. Then, a horse coming at blazing speed reached Stonehaven's walls. The archers were about to fire, but a voice stopped them.

"Hello there," said a deep voice. Ark noticed the trimming on the man's armor: gold trimmings and a nice hat. That can only mean one thing.

"My name is General Llyah, and our army and special guest will soon destroy this fine city. I'm not usually the type to give mercy, but I'm in a forgiving mood today. You have five seconds to surrender before my army lays a full assault on your base," he said threateningly. "But before that happens, where is the one who defeated Captain Mila?" he asked.

"Right here," said Ark, stepping up the wall. Llyah squinted and rubbed his eyes.

"Well, you're much more pathetic-looking than I thought you'd be." Ark felt his hands ball up in rage. Llyah pulled up his stat screen.

"HUH?!" he exclaimed. "Only level five?!" he asked, bewildered. "THAT'S IMPOSSIBLE! Come on man......no super cool gear? Not even one of those magic swords?" Well, it doesn't matter. I'll capture you and learn your secret eventually."

"What do we do?" asked Arvaan.

"We fight," said Captain Arthur, bashing his fists together.

"FIVE, FOUR," said Llyah, counting down. The soldiers were in a deep panic, commotion going around the wall. "THREE, TWO, ONE—ATTACK!" he yelled. Soldiers immediately began to rush, horses beating the ground. The archers let loose arrows puncturing armor across the battlefield. The dragon flapped its wings and flew across the battlefield.

"Cannon operators, fire!" yelled Daniel and Arthur. All six cannons struck the dragon directly, but the cannonballs bounced off its thick skin.

"Oh dear," said Daniel as the dragon approached closer.

"Ballistae, fire!" yelled Arthur. A few rounds shot off from the watchtower. All the ballistae were on target, but the dragon spewed flames from its mouth, incinerating the arrows and a few enemy soldiers beneath it.

"YOU STUPID BEAST, THOSE WERE MY FRIENDS!" yelled an enemy soldier. The dragon turned around and locked eyes with the soldier who said that.

"W-wait, I didn't mean it!" But it was too late; the dragon whipped the soldier with its sharp tail and sent him flying.

"Woah, that dragon has anger management problems," said Ark. "It's hitting its teammates." Ark had noticed some tiny green tents in the back of the army.

"Are they camping?" asked Ark, confused.

"They merely know there's a long battle ahead," said Captain Arthur, nodding. The dragon finally reached the wall, but it appeared to be lazy. It lay down without doing any damage to the wall or gate.

"HUH?!" said Ark, scratching his head in confusion. However, the dragon blocked the gate, acting as a defense. The enemy soldiers could not attack the gate because of the dragon, and no one dared to disturb it after what happened to the last soldier except General Llyah. He walked up to the dragon with a sword in his hands. It crackled with electricity.

"You had better obey me if you know what's good for you, you stupid beast!" Llyah said, striking the dragon with his electric sword. The dragon awoke with a jolt, roaring in pain. The dragon turned to see who had struck it, and as soon as it saw who had struck him, the dragon instantly had a look of fear in its eyes.

"Ah, so that worked. NOW TEAR DOWN THAT GATE!" said General Llyah. The dragon began to breathe fire on the gate. Unfortunately for the dragon, the gate was made of solid metal.

"Why isn't it just flying over?" said Ark.

"Because if it did, it would get pelted by ballistae. However, our ballistae can't reach it under the gate," said Captain Arthur.

"I have an idea," said Daniel. Everyone was paying attention closely. "The dragon doesn't seem to like electricity, and there's a lightning storm going on." As he said this, there was a strike of lightning. "And what attracts lightning?" he asked.

"Metal," said Arvaan.

"Exactly. If we lodge a metal arrow or something into the dragon, we may be able to attract lightning. The only problem is the dragon's out of sight, so we need someone to lure it. The chances it works may be low, but it's worth a shot."

Ark saw many of his teammates stomped on and burned by the dragon. "I'll do it," he eventually said. The mayor and everyone else looked at him.

"I'm the only one fast enough to lure it. I won't let that dragon hurt my friends," said Ark, feeling brave.

"Alright then," said the mayor. I have a way to get into the battlefield without the gate. Come with me," he said. Ark followed him down the steps into a small house. The mayor moved a bookshelf, which opened up a secret room.

"Woah," said Ark, quickly following the mayor down the stairs. They ran through the tunnel, and then there was a ladder.

"Good luck, Ark," said the mayor as Ark climbed. "You'll need it," he said.

12 HOW TO TAUNT A DRAGON

Ark climbed until he reached the top. There was a trap door. He climbed out to see a huge fight going on, and the sounds of swords clashing filled the air as he made his way through the thicket of the battle. Ark saw the dragon and General Llyah burning the gate down. It was a slow process, but it was working little by little. "The moles must be good at building," Ark thought. "The gate has hardly taken damage; they repair it so quickly." Ark ran towards the dragon and threw his old sword at it. "HEY UGLY, COME AND GET ME!" Ark said. The dragon was undistracted as it burned down the gate; however, it had caught General Llyah's attention.

"Oh?" he said, looking at Ark. "It's you, the one who defeated Mila."

"I have no business with you," said Ark, "only with the dragon."

"Unfortunately for you, I know what you're trying to do, and it won't work, not if I can help it," said General Llyah, thrusting his sword at Ark. Ark dodged, but a small piece of the sword managed to hit and pierce Ark's new armor. One small piece was enough to electrify Ark. He fell to the ground, paralyzed.

"ARGHH!"

"Are you so pathetic that you can't even fight me for two seconds?" asked General Llyah.

"A-Are y-you so p-pathetic that you need an electric sword to fight?" asked Ark, crawling.

"WHAT?!" yelled Llyah, outraged. "I'll have you know I just borrowed this for the dragon!"

"I thought you were so scary and commanding you didn't need it," said Ark.

"Only a fool would attack a dragon without proper protection," Llyah responded.

Daniel saw Ark on the ground, and he had moved General Llyah to a spot where the cannons could fire. So, Daniel fired a cannon at him. The metal ball flew straight and accurately, and it hit Llyah directly. There was smoke after the shot. When the smoke cleared, Llyah was still standing, his gold-trimmed armor unscratched, with a smirk. Ark and Daniel couldn't even believe it. The same cannon that had once torn up Captain Mila's armor was ineffective against General Llyah.

"Like it?" he said, pounding the armor with his fist. "It's an invention of Doctor Reivax. It allows the user to be virtually immune to heavy blunt damage. Still wrapping my head around how he did it," Llyah said.

"Ugh, this guy's annoying," said Ark, standing up. Llyah slashed him with the sword again effortlessly, making Ark fall backward. The dragon was still burning down the gate. The metal began softening as the dragon started pounding it with its tail. The battering Rams were getting through. The archers were not the best; the raiders reached the blind spot and hammered the gate. On the other side, a massive group of moles worked tirelessly to repair the gate.

"I'm getting bored," said General Llyah. "ROLL OUT THE CATAPULTS!"

"No..." said Ark faintly. He felt memories of past battles in his brain, all his fellow soldiers wounded. "Not the catapults." He felt a memory of a catapult crushing one of his allies. No, it could not be. Ark did not ever remember being in a battle like this or knowing any of these people, yet somehow, he felt a heavy emotion for them. The massive catapults rolled onto the field loaded with stones. Then they fired. The havoc wreaked across the battlefield; soldiers hit by the rocks were crushed and killed. Llyah had run off to control the dragon. Ark couldn't stand up, paralyzed on the ground. He saw a boulder being launched at him. It was on the trajectory to crush him.

"Well, it seems this is the end," Ark said miserably, "and I didn't even get to eat more carrots." But then, a figure jumped before him, breaking the boulder in half with a giant hammer. It was Arthur.

"Come on, kid, this isn't nap time," he said, helping Ark up. The two stood up and rushed the dragon; it was still pounding the gate. Then Llyah noticed the two of them and drew his electric sword. In a sudden turn of events, Arthur threw his hammer straight at Llyah. Arthur missed the shot altogether.

"Your aim is quite poor," said Llyah, laughing.

"That is a matter of perspective," said Arthur. There was a strike of lightning. Although he had missed Llyah, he had hit the dragon right in the face. The dragon stopped pounding and burning the gate and ran towards Ark and Arthur.

"Oh, dear," said Llyah, realizing he was in the crossfire. Ark and Arthur ignored Llyah and ran as fast as they could.

"RUN, BOY, like your life depends on it!"

"IT DOES!" responded Ark. The dragon stopped running and unleashed an onslaught of flames, roasting everything in its path, friend or foe. The smell of burnt grass rang through the night as the dragon stomped victoriously. However, Ark and Arthur had managed to get behind the corner of the wall, narrowly avoiding the flames. The dragon returned to its position, burning the gate down. However, a few ballistae fired at the dragon while it was on target. The dragon shrugged and burned all the ballistae bolts in midair. More archers aimed as it returned to its position; all their shots bounced off its thick skin.

"Tsk, we need to lure that dragon back here and give our ballistae a chance to fire," said Arthur, his voice analytical.

"Wait, where's Llyah?" asked Ark.

"Not sure, however, I get the feeling he survived the dragon," said Arthur. The battle was still going strong; the catapults had destroyed a few cannons, though, and the gate was about to break after constant battering. The situation was grim. Ark and Arthur picked up rocks and started throwing them at the dragon but to no avail. The enemy soldiers at the front blocked the shots with their shields. Meanwhile, Arvaan maintained morale with Sawyer and the mayor on the roof.

"DEFEND THOSE BALLISTAE WITH YOUR LIVES!" ordered Arvaan. Then, Arvaan saw the exact gold-trimmed armor figure.

"This battle doesn't seem to be going well for you. How about you surrender and save us all the pain?" bellowed Llyah, his words like knives at night.

"NEVER!" said Arvaan at the top of his lungs.

"Fine, have it the hard way," he said, smirking. "Either way, defeat is inevitable." Arvaan had a slight feeling he was right.

"I hope that Vortex City backup arrives soon," he said.

Ark and Arthur did their best to help their teammates, clashing swords with the enemy. Ark watched as his teammates were brutally slaughtered with no mercy. There was a flashback. Ark was standing all alone in a green grass field, all his teammates dead on the ground. Ark didn't know them like last time but felt terrible for them.

"No," he said, clenching his fists. Ark was snapped back to reality with a roar of thunder and a lightning bolt hitting the battlefield. Arthur noticed Ark's expression.

"What's wrong?" he said while fighting a soldier.

"Nothing," said Ark, bewildered at what he saw.

"Our numbers won't hold for much longer. We're losing drastically," said Arthur. Then Ark saw a figure in the distance: General Llyah. He had somehow survived the attack.

"Why do you look so shocked, Ark? You should have known it would take much more than that to scratch me."

"Looks like I made the mistake of letting you live," said Ark, dashing at him with his brand-new fancy sword.

"Ark, NO!" said Arthur, trying to hold him back. Llyah caught his sword midair and yawned, throwing it to the ground.

"Is that the best you have to offer, Ark?"

"You know what? I'll beat you without my sword," Llyah said. He threw the electric sword to the ground and raised his fists. Arthur and Ark both dashed at him, swords raised. Llyah smirked and threw them both to the ground.

"Argh, what class are you?" asked Arthur, pulling up his stat screen.

"Level 40 samurai," said Llyah.

"Ugh, that's how he's beating us. He's so much more powerful; all his stats are higher," said Arthur.

"Oh," said Ark. "That makes so much more sense now."

"I'm glad the idiot understands it, but I don't have time for school," Llyah said, drawing his electric sword.

"Hey, you said you wouldn't."

"I lied," said Llyah, rolling his eyes as if it were no big deal. He stabbed Ark in the back with his electric sword.

"AHHHHH!" said Ark, feeling the voltage and pain. The sword penetrated through his armor with ease. He did the same with Arthur, and both had massive wounds on their backs.

"Now, if you'll excuse me, I have a dragon to handle," said Llyah, swiftly leaving them on the ground. Arvaan was moving on the wall, instructing soldiers along with Sawyer, and Arvaan saw Ark and Arthur on the ground.

"NOOOOOO!" he said, looking at their wounds. "WE NEED A MEDIC HERE IMMEDIATELY!" yelled Arvaan. Amy was on standby and came to look.

"Oh no," she said, looking at the damage.

"We need to get down there immediately!" said Arvaan, surveying the damage. "Follow me here, Amy, and bring your best healing potions!" The two climbed down the secret entrance and then a ladder. They were now on the battlefield.

"Stick close to me," said Arvaan. They moved throughout the battlefield, the only sounds of catapults firing and blades clashing. The dragon was dead set on burning down the gate; the metal had melted a lot and was becoming soft. Arvaan and Amy made it to Ark and Arthur.

"Their wounds are severe, and they are paralyzed far beyond the aspect of traditional potions. At this rate, they will bleed out soon," said Amy concernedly.

"Why are you just staring at them?! Heal them already!"

"That's the problem," said Amy. "We only have one good potion and two injuries."

"So?" asked Arvaan. "Just pour half the potion in each wound, chop-chop."

"Afraid that to heal the wound, it needs the power of a full potion," said Amy.

"No..." said Arvaan. "You're not sayin'—"

"That's exactly what I'm saying," interrupted Amy, nodding sadly. "Only one of them will be allowed to live." There was a strike of lightning as she said this.

"No..." Arvaan fell to his knees. One of his good friends was going to die right now.

"I'll leave you the decision," said Amy, running off to help the wounded soldiers. There, Arvaan held the bottle in his hands, unsure of who to choose to live. Then suddenly Arthur got up, using all his strength, and saw the potion.

"Use the potion on Ark. He's the only one who can defeat the Iron Tyrant," Arthur said in a weak voice.

"What?!"

"It's true. Ark is no ordinary rabbit; he has powers, powers he will learn to control one day and defeat the Iron Tyrant. My time is up. Help your friend," he said, falling back down.

"He has powers?!" Arvaan said to himself.

But That was a matter for another time. Arvaan's look bounced from the potion to his friends. There only felt to be one option after what Arthur had said.

13 FALLEN

Arvaan poured the whole potion into Ark's wounds while Arthur lay on the ground motionless. In an instant, Ark's wounds began to close, healing rapidly. "Incredible." Ark awoke with a jolt. "Where am I?" Then Ark noticed Arvaan. "Hey, how did you get here?"

"You don't remember anything?" asked Arvaan. "You and Arthur fought Llyah."

Then the memories came back of Llyah stabbing him with his electric sword. "Llyah stabbed me!" exclaimed Ark.

"Now you're picking up."

"Well, wait till Llyah sees me. I feel even better than ever before. Also, where's Arthur?"

"About that…" Arvaan quivered his lip. "What?"

Then Ark noticed Arthur on the ground. He saw that he was motionless, and he saw his gaping wound. "No…"

"There was only one potion; one person could be saved," said Arvaan with a sad face. Ark dropped to his knees, at a loss for words.

"He wanted you to live," said Arvaan. "He sacrificed himself." Ark clenched his fist. "It's all my fault," he said quietly. Ark was now crying. "If I hadn't prematurely charged at Llyah, maybe Arthur would still be alive with us."

"We can worry—" Just then, there were flashes of lightning surrounding one point. A portal appeared. Arcs of lightning continued to ring through the night.

"What's this?" bellowed Llyah in the distance. "I didn't call for backup."

A figure emerged from the portal; it was Julia. "Maybe you didn't, but Stonehaven did."

"Wha-what?" said a very surprised Llyah. "What are all these rabbits doing here in a mole zone?"

"That's not just any rabbit; that's Mayor Julia of Vortex City," said what seemed to be Llyah's assistant. Colonel Ishaan and some soldiers poured out of the vortex and into the battlefield.

"Skip the pleasantries, Vortex City, CHARGE!" said Julia, her army having vigor. Just then, the dragon pounded the gate down. The gate had fallen with a groan.

"SOLDIERS ON THE GATE! WE MUST DEFEND IT!" Ishaan commanded. But little did Ishaan know he was leading his soldiers into a death threat. The dragon roared and let an onslaught of flames, but the soldiers defended with metal shields. Llyah engaged Ishaan, and catapults destroyed all the ballistae.

Ark and many other soldiers gathered around Arthur's dead body. "I still can't believe he's gone," said a soldier. Ark decided to tell the truth to the soldiers.

"Arthur was a great captain. He led his soldiers well and probably won many fights, but I'm here to tell you why he died this night," said Ark. People gathered around, anxious to know why. "Arthur died a hero; we fought against General Llyah, but he was just too powerful and over-leveled for us. He ended up giving us both major wounds with his electric sword. Then my friends came to help us, but they could only save one of us. Arthur sacrificed himself to save me."

Ark let it sink in, and all the soldiers started crying. Then, Mayor Julia came over to see what had happened.

"Ark? Is that you?" Then she noticed Ark's look. "Sheesh, who died and rained on your party?"

That was the last straw. "Died?" Ark began to cry loudly as tears streamed down his cheeks.

"Woah, woah, woah, I'm sorry. What did I do?"

"Arthur died," Ark said, crying.

"No…" said Julia, realizing what had happened. Julia didn't cry, but she looked defeated.

"Well, we can't cry over the past. Now we need to defend Stonehaven."

Just then, the dragon realized all the ballistae had been destroyed. With a roar that sounded like a laugh, it took flight and entered the city. Flying past the wall and the soldiers, the dragon began to burn down houses one at a time until everything caught on fire. The whole town was burning down.

"No... Stonehaven." All the soldiers watched their homes burn, and the civilians were trapped underground. It was only a matter of time before Llyah infiltrated the underground and captured the civilians.

"We've lost," said Ark, falling to his knees. As he said this, Llyah knocked down Colonel Ishaan, and his minions broke through the gates' defenses and went straight for the elevator, capturing as many troops as possible.

"We have to retreat! Find any survivors left and get them back here. We'll summon a vortex and get out of here!" said Julia, concerned for once.

"All right then." Ark ran into Stonehaven's gate, not knowing what to expect. There were flames everywhere; they had engulfed the whole city. Just then, one of the building's support beams crumbled from the fire, and a piece of the building hit Ark on the head, knocking him unconscious, and everything went black.

Arvaan noticed Ark on the ground, unconscious, and rushed to see what was wrong.

"Ark… I must get him out of here." Arvaan hoisted Ark on his shoulders and ran for the extraction point, but a few soldiers noticed them.

"Hey, they're trying to make a run for it! GET 'EM!" Arvaan ran as fast as he could, arrows blazing by his head. He saw soldiers defending the vortex point with barriers. Just then, Llyah spotted Arvaan carrying Ark.

"The boy lives?!"

Arvaan was moving too fast for Llyah to catch up, so he whistled for the dragon. The dragon emerged from the city at blazing speeds with a roar and was about to pin Arvaan down, but Arvaan threw Ark into the vortex right before he got pinned down. The dragon threw Arvaan's body back over the walls and into the city. Llyah banged his fist on the ground in anger.

"He may have got away this time, but our army will hunt you down to the ends of Viscland."

*

Ark awoke to medical equipment beeping and soldiers around him. The only familiar face was Sawyer.

"Sawyer!"

"Yes?"

"Where are we? What happened?"

"We lost the fight. We are at Vortex City now."

"Where's everyone?" Sawyer looked away.

"Where's the mayor and Arvaan?" Ark asked more urgently.

"All captured."

"No... First Arthur, now Arvaan and the mayor captured."

"They were all captured at Grim Keep," said Sawyer.

"The mayor told me about that place. Don't they capture people there?"

"Precisely. It's nearly impossible to raid because of its superior position on a mountain surrounded by oceans."

"I see. I'll raid that place and rescue everyone," said Ark confidently.

"Ark, that place is in a different league. You need to be at least level 40 to attempt such an attack. Besides, you'd need ten armies to raid that place. Everyone's given up; it's too secure."

"I'll get stronger. I'll find a way, for Arvaan's sake."

"I hope you do, Ark. I hope you do...."

EPILOGUE

"Scour the wreckage and leave no stone unturned!" ordered General Llyah.

"Yes, sir!" The soldiers responded in unison, hurrying to follow his orders.

"We will find that wretch Arvaan, and I will personally interrogate him about Ark. Somehow, I feel he's a hybrid. I must know his full powers." Llyah muttered, his eyes scanning the chaotic scene.

Then he noticed something: Arthur's body was gone.

"Peculiar," he muttered to himself. "It's fine. He's probably just around here somewhere." He saw a small group of soldiers capturing civilians.

"You there!" he barked. The guard instantly dropped what he was doing.

"YES, SIR!" the guard replied in a terrified voice.

"Have you seen any trace of Captain Arthur?" Llyah demanded.

"Why, no sir," the guard stammered.

Llyah continued questioning the guards around, but no one found Arthur's body. "AHHHH!" he roared, pulling his sword out and thrusting it into the guard's chest. The others watched in terror as the guard fell to the ground.

"So Arthur lives. I'm not sure how I'm not sure why, but he lives. No matter." He walked up to the nearest vortex mage. "You there? I require a vortex back to base!"

The mage quickly turned around and readied her staff. Arcs of white lightning began to bounce, and a purple portal appeared. Llyah walked in, feeling the relief of being back on the airship, sky-high above all threats. Initially, he felt dizzy but soon overcame it as he walked to the Elite room with the high-ranking officers. He noticed a soldier about to eat a fresh new pie.

"You there, don't eat that despicable stuff!" The guard immediately froze in her tracks. "I will be confiscating that," said Llyah, taking the pie out of her hands. The guard didn't say anything, afraid to get in trouble. Once Llyah walked far enough away, he began to eat the pie. "Skipped over breakfast, lunch, and dinner, and I'm starving," he said, devouring the pie. "This is quite good."

Then, a figure stepped into view from the shadows. He had a hat embedded with stars and a painted solar system. He wore purple robes that looked masterfully crafted. His pointed ears, tall stature, and translucent green skin marked him as the

Sylvanite, Wazzo Kabazo, the second in command of the army and the most annoying person on the airship.

"Stealing food again, Llyah?" asked Wazzo, leaning on a wall. Llyah tried to reply, but his mouth was stuffed with pie. He slowly swallowed. "Run on back to your next elite mission, Wazzo."

"I would, but they're all done," he paused for dramatic effect, "BECAUSE of me."

"Ugh, Wazzo, just shut up. I destroyed three cities; I don't have time for this. I have a pie to eat."

"So, you would rather eat a pie than talk to me?"

"Yes."

Wazzo growled. "Fine then, have it your way. I'm preparing to take down another city anyway."

"Don't fail too badly," said Llyah, running off. He could hear Wazzo banging his fist on the table as he ran.

Llyah then made it to the Elite room. He opened the door to see only Estreal, the fifth in command, present. She had purple curly hair and a mystical look. She was a rabbit recruited recently and much more likable than the Sylvanite, Wazzo Kabazo.

"Ah, Llyah, did you destroy those three cities I asked you to?"

"I did, in record time," he replied.

"Efficient as usual," responded Estreal. "However, there was a boy who attacked me. He failed, obviously, but there was something to him."

"What was wrong with him?" asked Estreal.

Llyah's lips curled. "I get the feeling he's a hybrid. He has powers. I know he does."

"Do you know where he currently is?" asked Estreal, her voice analytical.

"I'm sure he's in Vortex City now."

Estreal thought to herself and shook her head. "Unfortunately, Vortex City is quite strong. However, the hybrid boy is intriguing. I'll tell the big M about it."

"Good," replied Llyah, satisfied.

"Anyways," said Estreal, pulling out some schematics. "Llyah, this is our next target." Llyah leaned in close, listening to all the details. After an hour, he said, "Let's burn it to the ground."

ABOUT THE AUTHOR

Arush Gokul is a 13-year-old kid in middle school who loves video games, and he has been inspired by his favorite authors to write this book and he has had a lot of fun writing it.

Made in United States
Orlando, FL
18 November 2024